THIS CLOSE
TO HOME

ALSO BY BETH TURLEY

The Flyers

The Last Tree Town

If This Were a Story

THIS CLOSE TO HOME

Beth Turley

Simon & Schuster Books for Young Readers

NEW YORK   LONDON   TORONTO   SYDNEY   NEW DELHI

SIMON & SCHUSTER BOOKS FOR YOUNG READERS
An imprint of Simon & Schuster Children's Publishing Division
1230 Avenue of the Americas, New York, New York 10020

This book is a work of fiction. Any references to historical events, real people, or real places are used fictitiously. Other names, characters, places, and events are products of the author's imagination, and any resemblance to actual events or places or persons, living or dead, is entirely coincidental.

SIMON & SCHUSTER BOOKS FOR YOUNG READERS
and related marks are trademarks of Simon & Schuster, Inc.
For information about special discounts for bulk purchases, please contact
Simon & Schuster Special Sales at 1-866-506-1949 or business@simonandschuster.com.
The Simon & Schuster Speakers Bureau can bring authors to your live event.
For more information or to book an event, contact the Simon & Schuster Speakers
Bureau at 1-866-248-3049 or visit our website at www.simonspeakers.com.
Interior design by Hilary Zarycky
The text for this book was set in Adobe Garamond Pro.
Manufactured in the United States of America
0423 FFG
First Edition
2 4 6 8 10 9 7 5 3 1
Library of Congress Cataloging-in-Publication Data
Names: Turley, Beth, author.
Title: This close to home / Beth Turley.
Description: First edition. | New York : Simon & Schuster Books for Young Readers,
[2023] | Audience: Ages 8–12. | Audience: Grades 4–6. |
Summary: After the death of her mother, Brooke works to revitalize her town's festival
in hope that it will help her sister and dad heal and allow them to begin to move on.
Identifiers: LCCN 2022043956 (print) | LCCN 2022043957 (ebook) |
ISBN 9781534476752 (hardcover) | ISBN 9781534476776 (ebook)
Subjects: CYAC: Family life—Fiction. | Festivals—Fiction. | Grief—Fiction. |
LCGFT: Novels.
Classification: LCC PZ7.1.T875 Th 2023 (print) | LCC PZ7.1.T875 (ebook) |
DDC [Fic]—dc23
LC record available at https://lccn.loc.gov/2022043956
LC ebook record available at https://lccn.loc.gov/2022043957

For my parents

THIS CLOSE
TO HOME

CHAPTER ONE

THINGS SEEN BY THE FERNS

I have a job to do, and the sky helps me find my way. I rip off my catcher's mask and search the clouds for an electric-green foul ball. If it's anywhere behind home plate, my space to protect, then I'll drop to my knees in the dirt before I let it get away.

I lift my arm against the honeycomb-patterned fence, my glove finding the ball just in time. That leathery slap is my favorite sound in the world.

"That's three outs," the umpire announces.

My teammates give me high fives and pound on my chest protector when we swarm the dugout.

"Good one, Brooke."

"Nice out, Brooke."

I half smile at them and head to my corner, a place between the dugout and the fence where I store my equipment between innings. I sit on an upside-down orange bucket and sweep away the dark hair matted to my temples. Coach Tanaka calls this spot my Disaster Corner, but I know where everything is. Mostly. My bat is on the ground, and a torn bag of sunflower seeds spills out at my feet. My batting glove rests in the dirt like a seashell washed up on the beach.

I turn toward the fence and see my sister, Calla, cross-armed in front of a wall of ferns with her boyfriend, Robby. He stares at his red cleats while her mouth moves; I can't hear what she's saying, but it looks like *I'm sorry*. She leans her head toward the sky, and sunlight catches the wet spots on her cheeks. I look away, nerves racing around in my stomach like they do during championship games.

Mom used to say my focus made me a great softball player; nothing could get to me in the middle of the game. If she were here now, she wouldn't say that. Whatever I just saw between Calla and Robby burns itself into my brain. It's like I'm looking at the field through a filter of Calla's tears and green ferns.

"Helloooo." Lily Graham, our star pitcher, waves her hand in front of my face. She's the kind of pretty that everyone notices: gold hair, smooth skin. It's just a fact. She's Lily and she's the Pretty One.

"What's up?" I answer.

"You're up," she says in the not-exactly-nice way she says everything.

"Thanks." I grab a helmet and my sky-blue bat. I'm at the plate before I realize I forgot my batting glove. It's Mom's from when she played in college. There's a hole in the thumb and the Velcro is frayed, but I wear it anyway. I get into position at home plate, trying to push away the feeling that something is missing.

The pitcher on the other team, a girl from my homeroom with curly red hair, does her windup and sends the ball toward the plate. I swing so hard, I stumble forward. But the ball flies past me.

"Strike!" the umpire calls, as if I need the reminder.

I bounce the bat against my cleats while the catcher throws the ball back. Coach Tanaka motions to me from the third-base line. I look to him for a signal: maybe he wants me to bunt; maybe he wants me to swing no matter what. He doesn't give me the sign for either. Instead, he waves his hands and imitates a big breath. The sign for *calm down*. It's not a sign he's ever had to use for me. It only makes me more nervous.

The pitcher windmills her arm back again, and the ball comes at me. It's a little high, but I swing anyway. My bat slices through the air at nothing again, a bright blue blur.

"Strike two!"

I step back from the batter's box, hit my cleats with the bat a few more times. My heartbeat travels from my chest to my throat. It makes breathing hard.

"You got this, Brookie." Calla's voice comes from behind me. I turn my head. She's still by the ferns, but without Robby, smiling at me. It's not her real smile. It's the one she wore at Mom's funeral, when people came up to us one by one and said how sorry they were. A smile that looks glued on.

I get back into position. The pitcher wastes no time with her throw. It's a slower pitch, a changeup right down the middle, and I swing hard. My bat connects and the ball shoots into the outfield, over the center fielder's glove.

I run without thinking, head down, until I see the base under my feet. My hand throbs from batting without my glove. I look up from the dusty base and see Coach Tanaka, which doesn't make sense, because he was giving signals at third base, not first. Behind him, my teammates gawk through the fence that blocks the dugout.

I'm at third base.

I ran to third base instead of first.

"Go to first, there's time, back to first!" Coach Tanaka shouts, pointing across the diamond to the base where I should be standing. The center fielder has the ball now, and sprints across the outfield to make the throw to first. I run as fast as I can back down the baseline, touching home plate. Lily is slack-jawed in the on-deck circle. Calla has a hand over her mouth.

My feet pound the dirt and leave brown clouds behind. I'm almost to first when the center fielder's throw arcs across the infield all the way to first base.

"Out!" the umpire announces.

I jog back to the dugout, because it's important to hustle even if your heart is sinking. Lily continues to stare. I sit on my orange bucket and grab my shin guards from the ground where I tossed them. My teammates don't say it's okay, because it's really not. We are the Poppyseed Garden Center Lions, defending champions of the junior softball league. Errors like mine can cost us our first-place finish.

It's the second major error of my softball career. I may have a hard time keeping track of things, but I never forget my mistakes.

Luckily, we were already beating the J&B Funeral Home Bashers by three runs before my wrong-base debacle, so it doesn't ruin the game. Mom used to tell me that there is only one direction in softball—forward. You have to move on to the next play, the next game, no matter what. It's hard advice to follow. The thing about an error is it reminds me of all the other ones I've made, the ones off the field. And then I get stuck in the tornado of things I've done wrong.

For the first time in a long time, I'm glad the game is over.

CHAPTER TWO

EMERGENCY SLUSHIES

I gather all my stuff from the Disaster Corner and start shoving it into my bag. Coach Tanaka whistles through his fingers. The sound is like a wheezy bird.

"Listen up, Lions. Good work today." He pulls a stack of paper from behind his notebook, where he keeps track of the team's stats for every game. "I have permission slips for you. It's basically a release so we can help you in case of an emergency. You all turned this in at the beginning of the season, but we changed the template, blah, blah, boring junk. You won't be able to play until you get this filled out, so bring it back to me, signed, at Wednesday's practice."

Coach Tanaka hands out the forms. He pauses for an extra second when he gets to me.

"Don't think about what happened, Brooke." He gives

me my form. I wonder what he wrote about my error in his notebook. When he walks away, I shove the paper into the corner of my bat bag where dirty socks hide.

My sandals clip-clop on the path when I walk away from the junior softball field. To my right are some bleachers and the junior boys' baseball field. The senior fields are farther ahead, by the concession stand, and the football field is all the way up on the hill, goalposts standing like towers. I think I could walk through the fields blindfolded and not get lost. It's all as familiar as my own house. The Lincoln Youth Athletic Complex feels like home.

"Hey, B!"

I snap my head to the side. Derek jogs away from the junior boys' field with a bat bag bouncing against his leg. His red Papa Margherita's Pizza jersey is streaked with dirt. He takes his hat off, revealing black hair pressed down flat.

"Hey, hat head," I say.

Derek smirks.

"This is the hat head of a guy who hit three RBI doubles today. And look who's talking, sideburns."

I laugh and stuff the sweaty hair behind my ears. Derek catches up to me on the path. He rubs a palm hard against his head, and his curls pop up. It makes my heart pop too, but I try to ignore that. It's *Derek Perez*. Derek from the sandbox and front lawn sprinkler on extra-hot days. Derek whose abuela watched Calla and me when Mom went back to work. Permanent buddy-system Derek.

But lately he's been Derek who gives me heart pops.

"I ran to third instead of first, D," I tell him.

Derek gasps, then clears his throat like he's embarrassed. He puts his hat on backward. My neck gets hot but I try to ignore it.

"Emergency slushies?" he asks.

I nod and we keep walking. The hot dog smell hits me before we turn the corner to the concession stand, a white cement building with broken shingles on the roof. Smoke pours out of the little tin chimney. I spot Calla at a big wooden planter behind the stand. It's full of marigolds, though when we get closer, I can see they're mostly brown. The soil looks crumbly and cracked. Calla has the tip of her finger dipped in.

"What are they saying, Plant Whisperer?" I ask.

She looks up at me, smiles.

"Nothing that I can repeat." She takes her finger out of the planter and wipes it on her jeans. "No one is watering these. I told Mr. Spitz I wouldn't be able to help with the flowers as much, but now they're being forgotten," she says.

"Maybe you should've planted forget-me-nots," I say, and slap my thigh, pretending to crack up at my own joke. Calla humors me and half laughs.

"Maybe it'll rain," Derek says.

"That seems to be the only hope for these babies." Calla pats the dry soil over the hole she made.

"Or you could start coming to the fields like you used to. Bring them back to life," I suggest.

Calla squints at me. I know it's not an option. Her days are stuffed with student council, cooking club, Spanish club, anything to fill her time. She pulls car keys out of her back pocket. They're attached to a royal-blue lanyard dotted with daisies. Robby gave it to her for her sixteenth birthday. I think she stares at the keys for an extra second, but maybe I imagine it.

"I'm heading home. Do you want to come with me or wait for Dad?"

The mascara smudge under her eye reminds me of what I saw at the ferns. I want to ask about Robby, but maybe Calla won't want to discuss it by the wilting flowers. And I don't want to ask in front of Derek. He's kind of obsessed with Robby. I've caught Derek staring at him when we all watch movies together, copying his couch slouch and laughing whenever Robby does. I get it. Robby is a star outfielder and radiates with cool rays, like the sun. People with cool rays are usually meaner, like they're better than everyone else and they know it. But not Robby. Robby's energy is contagious. It feels special to be around him.

"We'll go with Dad. We require slushies," I answer.

Calla curls the lanyard in one hand and puts the other on my shoulder.

"You had a good game, Brookie," she says, her leafy-green eyes acknowledging that slushies are for tough times. "See you at home. Bye, Der Bear."

Derek rolls his eyes like he hates Calla's nickname for him, but I know he doesn't. For a second, Error #2 is out in the distance, so far away that I'd need a telescope to see it. I watch Calla's bronze-brown braid until she disappears into her little blue sedan, and Derek and I walk to the ordering window on the other side of the concession stand.

Dad is there, filling a white bucket with Dubble Bubble. His glasses are fogged up from the grill. Every parent in the junior softball and baseball leagues has to take turns working the stand. Tonight is Dad's shift.

"We need Cherry Explosions right away," I say.

"Uh-oh," Dad replies. "Haven't needed one of those since Derek ripped his pants sliding into home."

"Thanks for bringing that up, Mr. Dell," Derek says.

"Anytime. So what happened?"

I glance around the snack bar. Some of my teammates sit on the bleachers nearby, licking vanilla cones. Lily is with them. She's taken her tight French braids out, and her hair is all blond ocean waves that no curling iron could replicate.

"You don't already know?" I ask.

Dad's mouth straightens into a line before he turns toward the slushie machines. Sloshy liquid whirls around inside, red in one and blue in the other. He fills two plastic cups with Cherry Explosion.

"Calla may have mentioned something," he answers when he turns back around. My teammates burst into laughter over some joke I can't hear. Heat rushes to my cheeks, probably turning my face the color of my slushie. What if they're talking about me?

"I was distracted, I guess."

Dad snaps lids onto the cups and gives us each a paper straw (the stand made the switch to paper straws last season to be more environmentally friendly—it was Mom's idea). I take a careful sip of my drink. It tastes like a cherry wrapped in sugar and plastic, in a good way. Derek slurps away at his while Dad wipes slushie juice off the counter. Some parents barely fill your slushie cup when it's their turn in the snack bar, or they don't restock the Gatorade cooler when only the bad flavors are left (*cough*, purple, *cough*). Dad does it all. Sporting his cheesy grin and his favorite Baltimore Orioles cap.

Mom was like that too, but on a whole other level. No one ran the concession stand like she did. There was always plenty of blue Gatorade when she worked.

"Remember, it's just a game," Dad says to me now.

I grip the cold cup a little harder. Mom had a lot of softball advice, but that was the biggest. Whether I won or lost, hit a home run or struck out, every time, she would remind me that it was just a game.

"Thanks, Dad."

Derek and I walk over to the bleachers, on the other side from Lily, and sit down. A senior baseball game changes innings on the field in front of us. The sky is all kinds of pink, like swirls in the concession stand's rainbow sundae. Derek follows my gaze.

"It's cool that they did that," he says.

"Did what?" I take another sugary sip.

"I thought you were looking at the sign." He sucks up the last drops of his slushie. The straw wheezes.

The bronze sign is posted next to the ordering window, where Dad hands a senior player a hot dog. My head squeezes from brain freeze and something else. Something bittersweet.

"It is cool."

MADELINE DELL MEMORIAL CONCESSION STAND. Named for Mom. It's the first softball season without her. Last October, two months after Mom's funeral, the director of the complex called Dad and asked us to meet him at the stand. There was a purple suede cloth over the sign, and Mr. Spitz pulled it off like a big reveal.

"Wow, Phil. I don't know what to say," Dad said. He cleared his throat and adjusted his Orioles hat. "Maddie would love it."

"She was a staple here, Jonas. All you Dells are. With you helping out, Brooke playing, Calla watering our plants. We want to show our appreciation."

Calla hadn't looked away from the sign since Mr. Spitz had taken the cloth off.

"You named the hot dog shack after our mom?"

"Calla." Dad shook his head.

"They serve more than hot dogs," I added, because I didn't know what else to say. There was a softball-sized lump in my throat. It was wrong to be at the fields in the fall, when everything was brown instead of green. It was even worse to be looking at something named in Mom's memory. She wasn't supposed to be a memory. She was supposed to be here.

Calla's mouth dropped open, like she was horrified by what she'd said. "I'm so sorry, Mr. Spitz. It's nice."

It was just like Calla to apologize for having feelings. In that moment, looking at the silver sign with Mr. Spitz's fingerprint smudged in the corner, I tried not to have feelings at all.

The fluorescent lights above us turn on, pouring a white glow over everything, over Robby out in left field. Short black braids pop out from under his cap. I watch him punch the inside of his glove a few times.

"Why didn't Calla stay for Robby's game?" Derek asks.

"Not sure." I shrug. Derek studies my face.

"Want to tell me what was distracting you when you ran to third?"

"Not right now." I take a breath. Something is going on with Calla, and I ran to the wrong base, and Mom's concession stand sign makes my heart ache. But it's hard to feel too bad while watching a baseball game under the swirly sundae sky. "We got to play our favorite game today, D."

Derek smiles. He taps his empty slushie cup against my half-full one.

"That makes it a pretty good day, B."

CHAPTER THREE

GROUP PROJECTS

We're learning about bugs in science class. Or *insects*, rather. I sit in the back corner of the classroom on Monday, staring at the huge praying mantis image projected onto the whiteboard. Its twiggy green body stretches across the whole thing. I scribble notes on the page in front of me. The paper looks like my Disaster Corner in the dugout, or my side of the bedroom that I share with Calla—an explosion. I wish my binder could always look like it does on the first day of school, all empty folders and blank notebook pages. But now, in April, it's like a graveyard for old assignments and smudged doodles.

"These creatures are small, but don't let that fool you," Mrs. Valencia says. "Though they be but little, they be fierce."

Mrs. Valencia likes red lipstick and quoting things. She presses a button on her remote, and the screen switches to a list of facts about the praying mantis. I copy the slide word for word in the last bit of space on the page. Mrs. Valencia's tests are always pulled straight from her slides.

Kasey Maleski, the left fielder on the J&B Funeral Home Bashers, turns toward my desk.

"There's a fact missing," she whispers.

Aimi Tanaka, Coach's daughter and the second-base player on the Lions, scoots closer. The legs of her desk scratch the carpet.

"What?" she asks.

I lean closer but keep taking notes so I can get every line down before Mrs. Valencia switches the screen. My writing is so squished, I can hardly read it.

"Female praying mantises bite the male's head off after they *do it*." Kasey gnashes her teeth.

"Ew!" Aimi quiet-squeals.

I scrunch my nose. The fact makes my throat feel tight, like that movie on puberty we watched last year. The narrator tried to make the whole ordeal sound exciting, but to me it seemed more like a scavenger hunt with no clues.

When Mrs. Valencia has gone through all her slides, she turns on the lights and gives a stack of papers to the first person in each row, who takes one and passes the rest back. Aimi hands me my sheet over her head. The top of the paper says *Unit Project: Insects*.

"Now that we've gone through all the different orders of insects, we'll be moving into our unit project. You'll be working in teams of two to put together a comprehensive look at the insect of your choice. *Any* insect."

Keenen Porter, who sits in the front row, raises his hand. He wears his signature mischievous grin.

"Keenen, no black widows. We've been over this. Spiders aren't classified as insects."

"Aw, *maaan*." Keenen pouts and everyone laughs, including Mrs. Valencia. Kasey gets closer to Aimi and me again.

"Black widows kill their mates too," she says.

"Can we quit it with the mating jokes?" I snap.

Kasey and Aimi look at each other, then at me.

"Yikes, Brooke. What's up with you?" Kasey asks.

I'm not in the mood for jokes that make me feel confused, I want to say. *The idea of mating is scary enough without adding decapitation to it.*

"Sorry. Didn't mean to bite *your* head off. That was very black widow of me." I smile, and they both seem satisfied enough to turn back to the front of the class.

Mrs. Valencia explains the unit projects. We'll have to give an oral report and create a visual representation of the insect we choose. When she's done, she tells us to find a partner.

"While I'm coming around to your groups, please have out the classification sheet you completed for homework."

In the front left corner of the room, at the farthest desk from mine, Marley Macintosh raises her hand. The class quiets.

Mrs. Valencia calls on her. "Marley?"

"Can we work alone?" she asks. Her voice is sharp enough to give you a paper cut.

Keenen laughs, loud. Mrs. Valencia stares at him until he slumps back into his chair.

"Not for this project," she answers.

"No one wants to be her partner," Kasey mumbles under her breath.

It's mean, but I'm too panicked to think about that. My classification sheet is in my folder, unfinished. I told myself I'd do it before the game yesterday, but I didn't, so I said I would do it after the game, but I didn't, so I swore I'd do it on the bus ride to school. But I didn't.

Aimi and Kasey look at me.

"Me and Aimi, you and Larissa?" Kasey suggests.

Larissa from the Blossom Bakery Warriors usually sits with us in the back of the room, like it's our own junior league territory. The four of us pair up for any group project—even though some of us are enemies on the field, we're all allies in class. But Larissa is out today.

"Works for me," I say quickly.

Mrs. Valencia starts walking up to groups. She checks their homework and writes in her pineapple-printed notebook.

She approaches our corner.

"I'm working with Aimi," Kasey announces, and points to the completed homework on her desk. Aimi slides hers over too.

"What a surprise." Mrs. Valencia half smiles and writes in her notebook. "Which insect?"

"Fire ant," they answer together, laughing behind their hands at whatever best-friend inside joke they're thinking of.

"How about you, Brooke?" Mrs. Valencia turns to me with her pen ready. I feel a fire ant colony in my chest. I should go to the nurse, ask to have it removed.

"I'll work with Larissa," I say. I hug my binder closer.

"Larissa isn't here today."

"I know, but I'll text her after school to see which insect she wants to do. Maybe a centipede?"

Mrs. Valencia doesn't mark our partnership down in her pineapple notebook.

"And your worksheet?"

I glance at the empty lines where I was supposed to name bugs.

"I don't have it," I admit.

Mrs. Valencia doesn't look disappointed, but it doesn't matter, because I'm disappointed enough for the both of us, for the whole world. I feel like the worst person *in* the world. The classification sheet wouldn't have taken too long; I just kept putting it off until it was too late.

Mom used to have a system: the Do and Done baskets. As soon as we got home from school, we would put our homework in a pink plastic basket at the top of the stairs. The word *Do* was written on it in thick marker. Our worksheets and reading assignments moved over to a matching basket labeled *Done* when we finished our work, and Mom would make sure all the homework had made that journey by the morning. It helped me, to see the papers move from one place to another.

The baskets gathered dust behind the couch for a while after Mom's accident, and now they're in a closet somewhere. It was up to my jumbly brain to find the space to remember homework.

"This is the third week in a row, Brooke," Mrs. Valencia reminds me softly.

"I know, I'm sorry. It won't happen again." I grit my teeth with determination. It *won't* happen again. *No more mistakes.*

"Bring it in next class for partial credit." She turns to the other side of the room. "And work with Marley on the unit project."

I look toward the front corner, where Marley stares out the window. Coffee-colored hair falls to the middle of her back, fastened with a brown clip. Her sweater is like dark green seaweed.

"But she doesn't even want a partner," I say.

"No buts. Go join Marley and pick an insect." Mrs. Valencia walks to the next group.

"Yikes," Kasey whispers.

"She wants me to work with Bossy Floss? Seriously?" I ask.

"Don't look her in the eye," Aimi warns.

I know three things about Marley Macintosh.

1. She likes things done *her* way.
2. Both of her parents are dentists. They have a hedge trimmed to look like a giant tooth in their front yard.
3. She has locker number 73. I only know that because I have locker 72.

Everyone knows the first two facts, which is where the name Bossy Floss was born. I had gym with Marley last year. She once started a ten-minute argument over whether a volleyball had gone out of bounds (Marley's side: out; rest of class: in; result: the bell ringing before we could keep playing).

"Remember me fondly." I pick up my binder, walk to the window, and take the empty seat behind Marley.

She turns around slowly. She looks at me like we've never met, like we haven't been slamming our locker doors right next to each other all year.

"Hi . . . ," she says, the way a person might say "flesh-eating bacteria."

I clear my throat.

"Hi. Mrs. Valencia said we should work together."

She looks at me like I'm *covered* in flesh-eating bacteria.

"Great." Her binder is open, with the folder all clean and lined up straight. Purple tabs stick out from loose-leaf paper. I read the labels—*plants, cell behavior, insects*. I have the urge to hide my own binder. Everything inside is curled or creased or covered in stains from the junk that lives in my backpack. I don't have loose-leaf paper. I have a notebook pressed into the binder, one that can't even clip into the metal teeth.

"Your notebook is really neat," I say.

Marley rolls her eyes. "I hate group projects." She reminds me of a tree with her green sweater, brown bangs, stiff posture.

"Me too," I say, but I don't really hate them, because usually I get to work with my softball friends.

Marley looks surprised. Softer for a second.

"It's just frustrating to depend on other people for work you can do yourself." She exhales loudly.

"Totally." I think of that saying *don't poke the bear.* Better to agree with the bear.

"I'm sure we'll be fine." She looks directly at my grimy binder.

"What insect should we do?" I ask. When I flip past my overstuffed folder to the front cover of my notebook, it plunks onto the desk like a rock. "We could do cicada, honeybee, butterfly."

"Cockroach," she answers.

I squint. Mrs. Valencia hasn't spent much time going over the cockroach. Who would want to see that blown up on the whiteboard? And who would want to pick that bug for a project?

Agree with the bear.

"Cockroach is great."

Marley focuses on my binder again, but I don't know why, because the cover of my notebook is the least repulsive part of the whole thing. It's black with a baseball in the center and red roses blooming around it. Dad found it in a value pack at the Dollar Depot. He gave me a few and used the rest as guestbooks in our rental houses on Lincoln Lake, the lake homes Mom inherited from my grandpa Ed. She and Dad fixed them up and turned them into vacation rentals when Calla was two. I was born into helping with the houses, cleaning out the trash after someone stays, reading entries in the guestbook about people's time on the lake.

If Mrs. Valencia put up a slide about me, breaking down the anatomy of a Brooke, my brain would be made of softball, my heart full of Mom and Dad and Calla and Derek, and my lungs would be Lincoln Lake. The place where I feel like I can breathe the deepest.

"You okay?" I ask Marley.

She looks up. "Yeah. I've just seen that notebook before."

"At the Dollar Depot?"

The stranger stare settles back onto her face, making me feel like I should introduce myself. *I'm Brooke. Locker seventy-two. Please don't hurt me.*

"No."

She turns back to her desk and starts researching cockroaches on one of our classroom tablets. She doesn't speak to me for the rest of class.

On my way out the door with Kasey and Aimi, Mrs. Valencia calls me back. I freeze, turn, bump shoulders with Marley as I do. She glares and hurries past me. Keenen says "Bossy Floss" in a voice nowhere near a whisper.

"I just sent your dad an email," Mrs. Valencia says. "Let him know and have him respond. Thanks, Brooke."

My whole body reacts like to an electric shock—prickly skin, racing heart.

"Am I in trouble?"

Mrs. Valencia smiles. Her lipstick is a stop-sign shade of red today. "Not at all. Just have him email me."

I nod and leave the room, Mrs. Valencia's instructions still tumbling around in my head. *Just have him email me.* As if it were no big deal at all. Dad is already working at the accounting firm, taking care of the lake houses, bringing me to practices and games. Trying to remember to buy groceries to fill the fridge. All without Mom on his team. How can I add emailing my teacher to all that? How much can a person have on their plate before it cracks into a million pieces?

CHAPTER FOUR

WHERE THE GARDEN GROWS

After school, I find Calla in her garden. She's kneeling close to the edge and turning soil with her lavender shovel. Calla's garden was just a patch of dirt in front of the house until a few years ago, when she decided to make it beautiful with flowers and vegetables. She tells me it feels powerful to watch plants sprout from their tiny bulbs, all because she keeps them watered and facing the sun.

A small speaker plays Calla's favorite podcast. I can hear the hosts—two actresses from the medical drama she watches every Thursday.

"Hey," I say over the conversation about this week's episode.

Calla's shoulders leap to her ears. She flips around to face me.

"Brookie. You scared me." She presses the volume button until the speaker mutes.

"Sorry. Were you in the zone?"

Calla laughs a little. A tiger stripe of dirt crosses her cheek.

"You could say that. I left a snack for you inside. Garlic knots from cooking club."

The sun peeks out from behind our house, washing over Calla's face. My heart squeezes. When the sun hits Calla just right, she looks so much like Mom that I have to remind myself she's not, remind myself Mom isn't here anymore. And it hurts.

"Thanks, Cal," I choke out, and head for the front door.

Our house is a split-apart house. Well, the technical term is "raised ranch." There are two sets of stairs in the entryway—one going up and one going down. Calla's and my shared bedroom is on the upper level, past the kitchen and Dad's room and the bathroom with its yellow-and-black DANGER ZONE sign on the door. Dad thinks it's funny. Mom didn't think so, but she let him hang it anyway, like she let him fill the cabinets with Orioles-themed dishes and our walls with Orioles memorabilia. She would make jokes about having a yard sale for it all. But I know she loved our baseball-infused world as much as he does. They named Calla and me after famous Orioles players, Cal Ripken Jr.

and Brooks Robinson, and put baseballs in our hands as soon as we could grasp them.

But there was something they couldn't account for—on Calla's first and last day of T-ball, she stepped up to the plate, plucked the ball off its stand, and ran from the field, screaming "*LET ME HELP YOU*." Mom and Dad caught up to her on the junior baseball field, where she sat in a patch of dandelions, watering the yellow flowers with her tears.

Mom said Calla's green thumb grew that day. She's had it ever since. But now she uses watering cans instead of crying.

I take a garlic knot from the orange plate on the counter and shove it into my mouth on the way to my room. It's soft and butter soaked, like a delicious, greasy cloud. I wipe the oil onto my black leggings, take them off, and add them to the minefield of clothes on my side of the room. The laundry basket in the corner has a sign that says PLEASE, <u>FOR THE LOVE OF ALL THAT'S HOLY</u>, USE ME in Calla's square handwriting. But everything ends up on the floor. I find my coziest sweatpants, the ones with bleach stains and a hole in the knee, and pull them on.

Calla walks in wearing polka-dot socks.

"Need my sunglasses. I'm being blinded," she says. She looks to my side of the room, blinks like she's getting her vision back, then cringes at what she sees. "Brooke, I love you, but you *have* to put those clothes away."

"On it," I tell her, jolting from my spot. I hug heaps of clothes to my chest and dump them into the laundry basket. The mustiness makes my stomach sink—is this how I smell to other people? I throw the last sock in and observe my work. My side of the navy carpet is visible for the first time in days.

"See, took one minute. I'm fine with doing your laundry, but at least get it into the basket."

"I can do my own laundry." Guilt bubbles in my chest when Calla does the chores that Mom used to.

She laughs like I've said something funny. It feels like being stabbed in the gut. But the truth is, if I washed my own clothes, I'd probably flood the laundry room with soapy water.

"It's okay, Brookie," Calla says. She walks to the dresser on the back wall of the room—half is hers and half is mine. The top of my half has three foggy water glasses and some bobby pins; hers has plastic buckets of makeup and accessories, and a silver-framed photo of her and Robby by Lincoln Lake. I realize it's my first moment alone with her since yesterday. She was asleep next to her algebra textbook when I got home from the fields.

"Thanks for coming to my game. I know you've been busy," I say.

She sifts through one of her buckets.

"I try to be there," she says slowly. "Junior year is really important for college applications. I have to build up my extracurriculars."

Calla has said this a hundred times since the school year started. I try not to think about Calla leaving for college, because it makes me feel like someone stole the sun right out of the sky. And I can't worry about that darkness right now, because I need to ask her what happened by the ferns.

"I know. Didn't you want to stay for Robby's game, though?"

She finds her sunglasses and puts them on before I can read her eyes.

"Oh, webrokeup, but it's okay."

Calla is an expert at the positive-negative sandwich. In softball, that's when a coach is critiquing you but gives a compliment before and after the correction. Calla squishes the negative between the rest of her words so tight, you might not notice she said anything bad at all.

And these words seem especially bad.

"It's okay? You were together for so long."

She lays the photo of her and Robby facedown on the dresser.

"Yeah, it'skindofhardIguess, but things happen. Oh hey, make sure you do your homework."

How can she think about my homework when she and

Robby are over? Isn't she supposed to be curled in a ball listening to sad songs? Doesn't she want to scream? I could sit beside her, rub her hair while she sobbed herself to sleep.

"Calla . . . ," I start.

"And then set the table for dinner."

She starts to walk out, and I know our conversation is over. No crying, no comforting. Setting the table is my chore, because remembering to do it is easy. I mean, you either have the dishes on the table or you don't. It's not like dusting, where you can forget for a while, where you might not notice until the dust bunnies grow big enough to devour you.

"Okay," I say to Calla's back. "When do you think Dad is coming home?"

She pauses, then moves into the hall.

"I'm not sure. But I'll finish up outside and start cooking."

With Calla out of sight, it's too easy to imagine I'm hearing Mom talking, getting ready to make dinner.

My phone buzzes on my bed. Derek's name pops up on-screen.

> Was just thinking about you. Actually about
> your sideburns. So hi sideburns.

Something flutters behind my belly button. It feels scarier than usual, after what Calla just told me. I can't have boyfriend-girlfriend feelings for Derek. I can't lose my best friend over something like a crush.

You thought about me? Ew.

I send the message and hope it doesn't hurt his feelings. A cold breeze comes through the open window between our beds, touching my skin through the hole in my sweatpants. It gives me chills.

CHAPTER FIVE

FLAMiNGO-PRiNT WALLPAPER

Dad has an old truck named Gus. It used to be red, but it's more of a rust color now. The front seat is covered in stains that no cleaning product can remove. I kind of like them. They tell stories. Like the time Calla splattered a blackberry smoothie when a spider crawled over her leg. Or the time Mom soaked the armrest in hot chocolate when we were driving around looking at Christmas lights.

On Tuesday afternoon, Derek and I go with Dad to the lake, Gus's engine squealing the whole way.

"Which house are we going to?" Derek asks.

"Number twenty-five," Dad answers. He has the window rolled down and his arm hanging out.

I turn to Derek in the back seat.

"Flamingo House," I say. Derek and I refer to the houses by their qualities, not their numbers. Twenty-five has flamingo wallpaper in the master bedroom. Derek smiles. If he's thinking about my text from yesterday, he doesn't show it.

"That wallpaper was your mother's idea." Dad taps his fingers on the car door. "She wanted the renters to feel like they were in Florida."

I roll down the window and lean my head outside. The air is different at Lincoln Lake. It's clean enough to fix any messes you have inside. Mom once said lake air works miracles.

We reach the top of a hill, and the water comes into view.

"Who needs Florida when you have all this," I say to the glittering blue.

Dad turns into Lakeside Circle and drives slowly past the houses. Four of them are ours, the backyards all connected and leading down to the lake. He checks each one as we go. Two women sit on the porch at twenty-one (Purple Couch House) with glasses of wine. A trail of smoke hovers above the roof at twenty-three (Fireplace House). Twenty-five is empty and dark, and beyond that is twenty-seven (Skylight House), looking just as empty.

"Nice day in the circle," Dad says.

Nicer days in the circle fill my head: summer on the dock with Derek, Calla on Flamingo House's tire swing,

Mom and Dad pulling weeds in the backyards together. I inhale and hold the lake air in my lungs for as long as I can.

We park in the driveway of Flamingo House. The passenger-side door creaks on its hinges when I open it. Gus has as many special sounds as he does stains. Dad pulls two clear plastic bins out of the truck bed. He takes one, and Derek and I grab the other, holding either side.

"I can carry it," Derek says. The bin is overstuffed with sheets.

"It's okay." I act like it's because I'm strong and not because I want to stay close to him. His deodorant smells almost as good as the lake air, to be honest.

Dad types a code into the keypad. When the lock clicks, he pushes the door open and steps through the front door.

"Oh, come on!" Dad's voice is a roar.

I drop my side of the bin to stand by Dad, and Derek stumbles forward. My eyes scan the absolute train wreck left in Flamingo House. Bottles and pizza crusts cover every surface. I step over a tipped kitchen chair, and my foot lands in a sour-smelling puddle.

"Ew!" I try to shake the liquid off my shoe.

"Who would do this?" Derek asks. He drags the sheets into the entryway.

Dad breathes in deep. I'm surprised fire doesn't come out when he exhales.

"Brandon W and his four guests." He pinches the space between his eyebrows. "I hate Rent It."

Mom and Dad used to rent the houses just by word of mouth to people in Lincoln. We would host family reunions and birthday parties, and there was even a wedding once. When the Rent It website came out, Mom thought it would be a good opportunity for our family, and a chance to share Lincoln Lake with more people. Unfortunately, that includes people like Brandon W and his pack of party animals.

"Let us know what to do. We can help," I tell Dad.

Dad has a look on his face like nothing can help. He points to the bin of sheets.

"Can you fold those and put them in the master bedroom? Then strip the dirty sheets off the bed and bring them to the basement. I'll get started out here." He takes a garbage bag from the bin at his feet and shakes it out. The sound is louder than Gus backfiring.

"Sure." I nod at Derek, and he picks the sheets up again.

The master bedroom is at the end of the hall. We walk in, instantly surrounded by hot-pink flamingo print. When I look at the birds and the sunny glow from the window, it's easy to pretend this is a different day. A day when my whole family is here and the house isn't trashed.

"Is that . . . blood?" Derek asks.

I whip my head toward him. He's staring at the bed. A bright red stain explodes on the thick comforter.

"No way." I bring myself closer to the stain, wrinkle my nose, sniff. It smells like sweet berries. "Crisis avoided. It's juice."

Derek grimaces. "That's gonna be tough to get out."

"Let's hold off on telling my dad about it."

I tug the comforter off the bed and smoosh it into a ball, the stain hidden inside. Derek pulls a clean sheet out of the bin and starts to fold it in half. He folds again and again, but the fabric keeps slipping out of position.

"Does anyone actually know how to do these sheets with the stretchy parts?" Derek asks. His cheeks are a little pink.

I smile. It's like looking at a baby lamb—completely adorable. I shake the thought from my head. *Get it together, Brooke. It's Derek. Derek.*

"Fitted sheets." I walk over and take one side of the fabric. "Mom taught Calla and me how to fold them, but you need two people."

I smile and step back, and Derek does the same. The sheet hangs between us. I walk in closer to him, matching our sides of the blue fabric together. We copy the motion two more times. I feel like his face gets closer to mine with every fold, but maybe my mind is playing tricks. We finish the blue sheet and move on to the next one, yellow with thin white stripes. I step toward him again.

"B?" Derek says. Okay, our faces are *definitely* closer this time. The air is all Big League Chew breath and deodorant.

"D?"

The sound of glass bottles hitting the floor fills the house.

"You have got to be KIDDING me!"

Derek's eyes go wide. The sheet drops to the floor between us, and we run out to the living room. Dad grips a throw pillow tight enough to pop it. I would joke that the feathers will be another thing to clean, but Dad's face is like I've never seen it before: angry and teary-eyed. An almost-full garbage bag sits at his feet.

"They burned a hole in the couch. And covered it with a pillow," he says through gritted teeth.

Derek and I inch closer. I spot the golf-ball-sized crater in the cushion. It's black around the edges. My heart, still pumping from whatever just happened with Derek, seems to stutter.

"Dad, I'm . . . sorry," I say. I wish I could snap my fingers and clean the mess, stitch the couch cushion back together. I wish it didn't have to be Dad left to deal with the garbage and holes.

He squeezes the pillow between his hands. It has a

sequined palm tree on it. The idea of making the house feel like Florida suddenly seems hopeless.

"Take a bag and start picking up the trash from the yard, please," Dad says.

I look out the sliding glass door. The grass leading down to the lake is littered with cans and bottles. But we have to finish folding the sheets. And Derek has to finish whatever he was going to say to me.

"Dad, we can stay in here if—"

"Yard. Brooke. Please."

Derek takes two trash bags from the roll and hands one to me, and we rush out the door. The breeze gives me instant goose bumps. I shake out the garbage bag. The first soda can I pick up is crushed and smells like dirt. I follow the trash like a bread crumb trail out to the dock. Each house has their own. Flamingo House's is the shortest, made of chestnut-brown wood that creaks under my feet. I reach for another can and spot a frayed piece of rope looped around one of the dock's poles. It bobs up and down, carried by the water.

I'm in the memory before I can stop it.

On the hottest day of last June, two months before the car accident, we spent the ninety-degree morning cleaning out Purple Couch House. The trash bags were in a heap near the deck, and we were in a sweaty heap in the living room.

"We need to get air-conditioning," Dad said, and leaned back into the grape-colored couch.

"We need to get in the lake," Mom said. She lay on the hardwood on her stomach, one cheek pressed to the cool floor. Calla was in the same position next to her. I sat near the sliding door to the deck, resting against the glass.

"We don't have bathing suits. We'll get our clothes all wet." Calla rolled over, turned herself into a star.

"We're already soaked in sweat! Better Lincoln Lake water than our own bodily fluids."

I scrunched my nose, half grossed out and half happy that I had the kind of mom who made jokes about bodily fluids. She looked at me eagerly, like a puppy who wanted to play. "You in, Brookie?"

"Last one there has to remake the beds!" I threw the door open, claimed my head start down to the dock. When I looked back, Calla was right behind me, then Mom, then Dad, who I knew would follow Mom anywhere.

"Jonas, catch!" Mom made a sudden turn toward the side of the house, where a set of black inflatable tubes was stacked up. She threw two toward Dad and then rolled two of her own down to the dock.

The water was sweetly cold on my skin. Calla dunked her head under. Mom got the tubes into the lake and told us to get in, so we each climbed up onto one. Mom paddled over to me, *which was more like frantically slapping the water for momentum, and then gripped the handle on my tube.*

"Now you hold on to Calla's," she instructed.

I reached out for Calla's tube, and she held mine. Mom got hold of Dad's on the other side. We were all connected, like one floating organism. We drifted a hundred feet from the dock before any of us realized it.

We called it Mega Float, and a few weeks later we did it again, this time tying ourselves to the dock. But it wasn't the rope that made me feel tethered to something safe. It was my family.

I turn away from the tattered rope reminder and hurry back up the dock, cans shaking around in the garbage bag. Derek is standing in the middle of the yard.

"I didn't think anyone was staying in Skylight House. It's so dark in there." He points his chin toward the water. I turn and see a girl with dark brown hair at the end of Skylight House's dock. I've been too caught up in the memory of Mega Float to notice her. All I can see is the back of her head, and a sweater the color of the water. She looks familiar—well, as familiar as a silhouette from a distance can look.

"Is that Marley?" I ask Derek.

"Who?" His trash bag whips in the wind.

I sigh, pick up another crusty can.

"Bossy Floss." I lean my head toward the lake. It feels kind of wrong to call her that now that I've actually talked to her, now that I've seen what her face looks like when it's not angry. Even if she did take over our insect project.

"Oh." Derek looks at the dock. "I can't tell. But I don't really know her . . . you know?"

"Yeah, me either."

Derek walks to the other side of the yard, toward the fire pit, which is full of Burger King bags. I don't know what kind of moment was building between Derek and me in the flamingo room, but it's blown away now. Part of me is glad, and another part desperately wants to know what he was going to say. We pick up sticky bottles until the yard is clean. The sun starts to go down, and Dad calls us back inside; the girl down on the dock doesn't move.

CHAPTER SIX

THE WRONG KIND OF CHANGEUP

L ions practice starts at four thirty sharp on Wednesdays. Calla drops me off on her way to her algebra study group. Her car doesn't have a name like Gus does, but it still has its own personality. The radio volume won't go up or down. It stays at level twelve always, which is loud enough to hear clearly but soft enough to still have conversations over. A happy medium.

We listen to her podcast on the way.

"Look, we know you're upset about the Donna and Jay breakup," the host with the Southern accent says.

"Don't take it out on us, listeners," the other host says. She sounds like she has a cold. *"We didn't write it!"*

Calla clears her throat and unplugs her phone from the auxiliary cord.

"Are you devastated about Donna and Jay too?" I ask. She half smiles.

"Haven't seen this week's episode."

We pull into the athletic complex, and Calla's knuckles go pale on the steering wheel. Her eyes shift to the senior boys' field when we pass. I watch her grip loosen when she sees that it's empty.

No Robby.

I climb out of Calla's car, grab my bat bag out of the back seat. It leaves dirt on the suede.

"Be good, Brookie," she says. She cranes her neck to look back at me. The sun touches her cheek and she's Mom again, repeating what Mom always told me before practice. *Be good, Brookie.* Not only has she taken over Mom's chores, she's also assumed the Brooke Encouragement duties.

But I don't want Calla to keep morphing into Mom. I want her to be the sister I can tell non-parent-approved secrets to, like what happened in the flamingo room with Derek and how it made me hot all over like a sunburn. If I told her about it now, she'd probably sit me on the bed and discuss my *CHANGING BODY.* Or she'd be too busy with her clubs to say anything at all. I close the car door too hard, and Calla takes off.

The dugout is buzzing when I step in. My teammates are slipping on their cleats and tightening their visors. A row of bat bags hangs on the wire fence, shaded by the slanted roof. I smell the cut grass, see the diamond shape of the white baselines. Field air fills my lungs the way lake air does—light, easy. Coach Tanaka is waiting in the outfield to start our pre-practice meeting. A semicircle of players sits around him.

"How's your unit project going?" Aimi asks when I plop down next to her. She has on a shiny black visor that matches her hair.

"Good, I guess?" I dig my fingers into the grass underneath me. In class earlier, Marley showed up with poster board and craft supplies and printed pictures of cockroaches. I followed all the instructions (more like orders) she gave me. "Marley's basically doing everything. She's probably finished it by now."

Marley keeps our conversations strictly to cockroaches, and only within our science classroom. She didn't give me any openings in class or at our neighboring lockers to ask if she was the girl on the dock. I guess it's kind of a weird question anyway.

"Did you know she's staying in one of your lake houses?" Lily sits down. Her hair is tied up with a red ribbon. Lily's family rented Fireplace House for a graduation party once. Not that it made us friends or anything.

"Really?" I ask.

Lily blows a pink bubble with her gum and it pops all over her mouth.

"My mom told me. Apparently, her mom left her dad. You know that tooth hedge in their front yard?"

I nod, and Aimi does too, quick like a bobblehead. The tooth is something of a landmark in Lincoln. People from out of town drive around the Macintoshes' cul-de-sac to see it.

"Her mom took a chain saw to it and split it right in half!"

Aimi lets out a squeaky laugh even though it isn't funny. But that's just how people act around Lily. Like worker bees trying too hard to please the queen.

"That can't be true," I say quietly.

Still, I think I saw Marley on the dock. And she said she'd seen my baseball notebook somewhere before, the same one we use for guestbooks. The story makes me feel like *I'm* getting split with a chain saw. When Mom died, it seemed that all of Lincoln knew, like Dad and Calla and I had neon signs hanging over our heads. *Look at these people. Don't they look devastated?*

"Of course it's true. That's the Messy Macintoshes for you."

Coach Tanaka clears his throat and we all snap to attention. He flips to a new page of his notebook, then turns it around to show us. It's totally blank.

"What is this?" he asks.

"A stats book," guesses Sophia Cruz, our center fielder and backup catcher.

"No. Well, yes. But no."

"Paper?" Aimi asks. Coach Tanaka smiles. Usually, you can't tell that Aimi is his daughter, because he treats us all the same no matter who we are or how well we play. But sometimes he slips up and claps extra hard for her.

"No." He holds the book higher. "This is a fresh start. Anything that happened during our last game is in the past. We only look ahead."

The grass is spiky on my bare thighs. I tug on a thread coming loose from my high sock. He doesn't have to say what he means. Errors are in the past. Including *my* error.

"And ahead is the championship tournament. We have to stay sharp until then. Sound good, Lions?"

"Yes, Coach," we answer in unison.

"Good. Let's start with stations. Outfielders, you're taking fly balls. Infielders, work grounders. Lily and Brooke, go throw. At least twenty pitches."

Coach Tanaka claps, his way of saying our meeting is over, and we break into our assigned stations. I jog to the dugout to put on my shin guards and helmet. I don't have to put on my full gear for practice pitches, but I definitely don't want to be unarmed. I ended up with a grapefruit-sized bruise on my shinbone last time I went without any protection.

When the Velcro on my shin guards is fastened tight and I have my catcher's mitt on, I meet Lily at the spot along the fence where we take practice pitches. She has a lime-green ball in her hand. *Lily G* is written in marker between the red stitches.

"I want to do changeups," she tells me, blowing another bubble. "And I want to switch our fastball signal from two thigh taps to one."

"Why? Coach Tanaka set those."

The bubble snaps between her teeth. She grips the ball tighter in her hand.

"Coach Tanaka isn't the one on the mound."

Sometimes when I talk to Lily, I get distracted by how smooth her skin is. No way she's ever had to scrub her nose with blackhead remover. She's the prettiest girl I've ever seen in person, like a star from Calla's medical show in real life. Around her, I become just like all my other friends, a bee buzzing helplessly for her approval. I wonder what made us all decide that it means everything for Lily Graham to like us.

"One tap it is." I pull my helmet on, and the mask part covers my face. The black bars split Lily into pieces. She grins and tosses her ball in the air, then snatches it in her glove like she's a Venus flytrap.

We stand about forty steps apart, which is how far away she'd be if we were in our real spots on the field. I hold up my mitt, stretch it wide, then squeeze it shut. Stretch, squeeze, stretch, squeeze. I repeat the motion three times. The helmet presses into my ears and lowers the volume of everything: teammates in their stations around me, the wind blowing through the trees, my thoughts.

I squeeze my mitt again to signal to Lily that I'm ready for her to start. She nods. I tap my thigh, just once, to tell her to throw a fastball. She winds her arm back in a three-hundred-sixty-degree circle, then lets go of the ball right around her thigh. It cuts through the air in a straight line, aimed directly at me. I track it until it's tucked safely in my mitt. The impact stings in the best way.

"Nice," I say. I toss the ball back to her. She flips her hair.

I do a small circle with my finger to tell her to do a changeup. Her arm flies back, but this time it slows down as she approaches her release point, and the ball moves at a lower speed than usual. Batters get confused when they think you'll throw a fastball but instead do a slow pitch.

They usually end up swinging at nothing. I have to be patient when Lily throws a changeup, wait for the ball to arrive at the plate.

On the other side of the field, I see Mr. Spitz enter through the gate. He's wearing a polo, swishy track pants, and white sneakers. Coach Tanaka throws a pop fly to our left fielder before meeting Mr. Spitz near the pitcher's mound. They talk for a second, and then Coach Tanaka cups his hands around his mouth.

"Bring it in quick, Lions!" he shouts. We all stop and hustle over, then huddle around him.

"What's the issue?" Lily asks sharply. She slaps the *Lily G* ball into her glove.

"The *issue*," Coach Tanaka begins, "is Mr. Spitz has reminded me that I need those emergency forms from you. Go grab them and we'll get back to work."

I don't follow my teammates to the dugout. Because I know where that form is: still crumpled up in my bat bag, unsigned. I forgot, *again*, to be responsible. And that feeling is heavier than my catcher's gear.

"Brooke?" Coach Tanaka asks.

"I forgot the form, Coach," I admit.

Coach Tanaka looks at Mr. Spitz, who looks at me. His expression is the same one he wore the day he showed Dad,

Calla, and me the sign on the concession stand. Too much sympathy. Like his words might break us.

"You won't be able to play or practice until you get that taken care of. Sorry, Brooke."

Lily's sigh comes from behind me, loud and exasperated. She shoves her form toward Coach Tanaka.

"I really wanted to practice my changeup more," she says.

"Rules are rules," Coach says. "Sophia will step in."

I want to squeeze my helmet tighter to my ears, to distort the sound of what's happening. No playing? No practice?

"Sorry," I mumble, partly to Coach and partly to Lily, who turns on the heels of her pink cleats and stomps to the fence. It occurs to me that Lily kind of *needs* me. I know her pitching style and signals. But that's not enough to put me on her level of the social pyramid. Or to get me out of this situation.

Coach Tanaka puts a hand on my shoulder. "Hey, sometimes I forget the milk's expired till I take that first sip."

I laugh. It's the first time spoiled dairy has ever cheered me up.

"Bring it to the game Saturday," Coach says. "Watch from the dugout for today."

I jog off the field, because it's important to hustle no matter how bad your time on the field went, and take a spot at the end of the bench. I keep my shin guards on.

Mom's softball advice fills my head, *it's just a game* shouting louder than the rest. It should be okay to miss one practice. But it's not just a game to me anymore—it's a link to Mom, and to life when she was here, cheering from the bleachers or swirling slushies in the concession stand. I can't break the link.

The sky is turning pink when Coach Tanaka calls the team into the final huddle. I watch my teammates put their hands into a circle.

"Lions, let me hear you!" Aimi shouts.

"Raaaaaaaaawr!" the team shouts back.

"Rawr," I say to the dusty ground.

I'm out of the dugout before the rest of my team, just as Gus pulls into a parking spot near the field. The passenger-side door has three softball-sized dents from throws that went out of control—one from Derek, two from me. I toss my bag into the truck bed before getting in.

"How'd it go?" Dad asks as I buckle my seat belt. He puts the truck in reverse, and the tires whine.

My throat feels dry. I know I need to tell Dad about the form. But I hate letting him down. When I think about

Dad, I think about second-base throws. It's one of the most important duties of a catcher. When a runner is trying to steal second, the catcher throws the ball over the pitcher's head to second base to get the out. The pitcher has to duck out of the way, like how Dad has to duck and dodge the obstacles of raising Calla and me without Mom.

I wish I made it easier on him.

"It was good," I say, too fast. "But can we go?"

Dad looks a little suspicious but keeps driving out of the parking lot. I want to steer our conversation, and Gus, far away from practice.

"Dad, are Marley Macintosh and her mom staying in Skylight House?"

"Which one is that, again?"

The inside of the truck is dim, but I can see the corners of Dad's mouth turn up. I laugh and roll my eyes.

"Are they? She's in my grade. Lily said her parents are separating and they're—"

"Yes, they're guests. But it's not nice to spread rumors, Brookie."

Calla's voice, or maybe it's Mom's, whispers in my ear—*Be good*. But I haven't been good at all. I forgot to get my permission slip signed. I let Lily gossip about Marley.

"Sorry, Dad."

A clunky sound from under Gus's hood fills the silence on the rest of the ride home.

I don't tell Dad about the form. Later that night, after Calla falls asleep, I take it into the bathroom and forge Dad's signature.

CHAPTER SEVEN

ASSIGNED SEATING

Marley and I stand next to each other at our lockers at least three times a day in the few minutes between classes. On Thursday between first and second periods, I glance over at her more than I ever have. More than I should to not look creepy. Every time she moves the door enough for me to see her face, my mouth fills with questions. *Do you like Skylight House? How long did you stay out on the dock the other day? Now that we're working together on this project, don't you think you should at least talk to me?*

She's back behind the door before I muster up the courage to speak. The same thing happens in the time between second period and lunch. It almost feels intentional, the way Marley doesn't look at me. Or maybe it's just normal. It's not like we've really talked at all this year. Other than this cockroach assignment, the last interaction I had with Marley was during that volleyball game in gym class. She turned her attention to me in the middle of her ball-went-out-of-bounds argument and snapped, "You saw it go over the line, right?"

Honestly, I had no idea whether the ball was in or out, but it was clear from the faces of the rest of the class whose side I was supposed to be on.

Marley shuts her locker and walks away just as Derek and Aimi come out of the math classroom nearby, in the middle of a laughing fit. Heat sweeps through me like I witnessed something I shouldn't have. Something I didn't *want* to see.

Derek stops next to me, mid-grin. Aimi waves and says she'll see us in the cafeteria. When Derek actually looks at me, his smile drops.

"What's wrong?"

"Is Aimi your best friend now?"

I feel foolish the second the words leave my mouth. Derek must find them funny too, because he looks like he might laugh again.

"No, that's my best friend." He points to a picture hanging in my locker from a llama magnet. It's a blurry picture at the lake. Someone's finger covers the frame in the corner. But everyone is there—Mom and Dad, Calla,

Derek's mom and abuela. Derek and I are five years old, standing in the front with our arms looped around each other's necks. I don't remember when it was taken, or why we were all together, but our faces are cheerful blobs.

"She looks fun." I close the locker on our happy memory.

He nods. "She definitely is. And a lot of other things too."

I start walking before he can see my face turn red, before I break and ask him what other things I am. *It's Derek. Chill.*

I've calmed myself down by the time we get to the cafeteria. Derek and I always eat at a long table with the school sports teams. We sit at one end with Kasey and Aimi and some baseball players, the lacrosse team takes the middle, and Lily's group sits down by the windows. It reminds me of the way insects are categorized—everyone falls into an order. On our way to our seats, I spot Marley at a table by the vending machines. She must have sat there all year. But I never noticed the way she and the two others at the table sit feet apart from each other, in the same space but eating alone.

The discovery gnaws at my chest.

I think of a whole new set of interview questions for her, if I ever get the nerve to talk to her about something other than cockroaches. *Did your mom really cut that hedge in your yard in half?*

Maybe I'd tell her that on a Sunday morning two years ago, my mom was reading the paper at our kitchen table, and I was eating pancakes in the spot across from her, when she jolted from her chair. She spun the paper around to face me. The pages made a crinkly sound.

"Look," Mom said. "Lincoln has a landmark."

She pointed to the picture of the tooth shrub in Marley's yard. The paper had run an article on it, with the headline QUIRKY LANDSCAPING DETAIL ATTRACTS AN AUDIENCE.

"But that's just a normal house," I said.

"It's no normal shrub, though. Let's go see it."

Maybe I'll tell Marley that Mom and I drove to her house with the radio on loud, and when we got there, the cul-de-sac was full of other cars. One by one we drove past the tooth, and more cars piled up behind us, and I couldn't believe how much of a spectacle that small, leafy molar had become. But Mom was next to me, and with her, even trips down the street felt like an adventure.

I guess the hedge is still kind of a spectacle.

Are you glad the tooth is gone? Is it sliced to shreds, or is any of it still standing?

CHAPTER EIGHT

WHY ARE YOU DOING THIS?

Derek takes the bus with me after school so we can watch the Orioles game together at my house. We haven't talked about Flamingo House at all. Instead, we cover whether our teams will make it to the championships (fingers crossed we both do), what Calla's cooking tonight (unknown, but she said she'd kick my butt if I didn't unload the dishwasher before dinner), and Derek's abuela misplacing her hearing aid (he's basically lost his voice from screaming). It's normal and easy in our D and B bubble. No heart pops detected.

We get off the bus at the top of my street and walk down the short hill. My house comes into view through our neighbor's trees. I see Calla and Robby on the front steps. I slow down and Derek runs into me. His shoulder nudging mine bursts the D and B bubble and leaves my skin flaming again. He moves away, and all I can think is how I don't want him to. *Stop! It's DEREK!*

"Why'd you freeze like that?" he asks.

"It's Calla and Robby." I motion toward my house.

"Oh, awesome." Derek picks up his speed. I reach out and grab his arm, ignore the lightning-bolt feeling in my fingertips.

"No, not awesome. They broke up."

He whips his head toward me, his mouth a horrified O.

"What?" Derek looks like he's the one who got broken up with.

"Yeah, on Sunday at the fields."

"Why didn't you tell me?"

"Because I knew you'd be devastated." I half smile so he knows I'm kidding.

He rolls his eyes and tugs on his backpack straps. I feel bad for not telling Derek. But it didn't feel like my news to tell, when I really don't even *know* what happened.

We stop in the driveway near Calla's garden. I consider our options: stay out here or walk past them to the door. The two seem equally awkward.

"I just don't understand," I hear Robby say. "I want you to tell me why."

Calla notices us and waves her hand like *shoo*. But where exactly does she expect us to go?

"Hey, Robby," Derek calls, waving. Calla puts a hand over her face. Robby turns and gives Derek a little salute. His eyes are glassy and red.

"Come on, superfan," I say.

I lead him around the house to the back porch. I tug on the sliding door a few times, but it doesn't budge. Locked. The kitchen window is next to the door. It doesn't have a screen. Maybe I can manage some acrobatic skills and climb through. The window wiggles a little, like it wants to open, but it's locked too.

"Let's go spy," Derek suggests.

"No way, it's private," I say, but I can't deny that I want to know what they're saying.

"Calla will tell you about it anyway, I bet. You're just getting a jump start." He tiptoes down the porch steps. His curls blow around in the wind.

My heart pinches, because I know she won't tell me. She's been too preoccupied with school and clubs and pretending to be Mom to share anything but a bedroom with me.

"Okay, let's go."

We creep around the corner, sit with our backs pressed against the house. Calla's voice is clear.

"Stop trying to make me explain." She sounds exhausted, like when she gets home after having two clubs in one day.

"I don't want to make you do anything, Calla. But we've been together for four years. Don't you think I deserve a reason?"

I met Robby for the first time at the lake. It was May, the start of the busy season for the houses, and Calla and I were avoiding cleanup-day chores in Flamingo House's front yard. She was twelve and I was eight. I tossed a softball up and down while Calla wrote in her journal. The sound of a bicycle bell cut through our quiet. Robby stopped his bike and leaned it against the massive oak tree in the front yard. He had a basket on the front with a stuffed poodle in it. Calla beelined to the tree, stopped a few feet from Robby, and started twirling her hair. Robby reached into the basket and handed Calla the poodle. She hugged it tight to her chest.

After that day, a lot of our family's memories started having Robby in them.

I lean as close as I can toward their voices. Since I can't see them, I picture Calla and Robby as their younger selves, all smiley and squeezing stuffed animals.

"There is no reason. Not everything has a reason. Things just happen," Calla says.

I flinch for Robby. There has to be a reason. Otherwise, wouldn't you spend your whole life wondering why? What if? That sounds unbearable.

"Calla," Robby says her name slowly. "If you're doing this because you're hurting, let me help you."

Her words snap into place. *Not everything has a reason.* Things like Mom being here one day and gone the next, things like a driver running a red light and slamming into the side of her car. I wait for Calla's response, but there's only the zip of the wind in my ears, and Derek breathing next to me.

"But if you're doing it because you're really done with me and you don't love me, I won't bother you again."

Calla's plants bow in the garden, almost like they're eavesdropping too. I picture Calla's arms wrapped around the poodle like she'll never let it go.

"Just leave. Please."

Robby makes a crackling sound in his throat. When he's walked far enough from the house, I can see him from our spot. His bike is leaning against a tree. It's not the same bike as that day at Flamingo House. This one is motorized. There's no bell, no basket. Robby is different too—two feet taller, his dark brown arms doubled in size, braids instead of a buzz cut. He disappears down the street.

"Move!" I whisper-yell at Derek.

We scramble to the porch like we're running the bases. If we don't get there before Calla gets inside, she'll know we were listening. Which might be worse than getting called out at home plate. I hear the front door close as we climb the stairs and drop into wooden chairs. My breathing is heavy when Calla appears, but I hide it. Derek leans back in his chair like he's been relaxing for hours. She clicks the lock and slides the door open.

"Hey, you two, sorryyouhadtoseethat, come inside."

She buries the apology inside her sentence. Her conversation with Robby sounded so hard, but she's acting like it didn't happen.

"What was going on?" I ask.

Her eyes squint a little, and for a second, I think she might tell the truth.

"It's nothing." She smiles her glued-on smile. "I have to run some errands. I'll be back."

Calla turns on her heel. I think about Robby riding down the street on his bike, his head full of the same questions rattling around in mine. Did Calla really stop loving him? Or is she hurting?

And if they can go from seventh graders with crushes and poodles to broken-up teenagers, will that happen to Derek and me? I can't lose him; I've already lost Mom, and Calla will leave me for college soon. I won't do anything to put my friendship with Derek in danger. Especially something as scary as falling in love.

Perfect

Before my parents started using Rent It, before the internet world could search for our little spots on Lincoln Lake, there were times when Lakeside Circle was empty. On those nights Calla and I got to pick which house we wanted to have dinner in as a family. My favorite was Flamingo House, and Calla's was Purple Couch, so we tried to take turns with the choice. But Calla liked to play the older-sister card. I let her, because as far as older sisters went, she was a good one.

A few months after Robby came by with the poodle, we decided to go neutral and pick Fireplace House. Mom was curled on the couch with a novel, and Dad was on his way with Papa Margherita's pizza. Calla suggested we hang out on the dock until he got there. I remember the surge of coziness, the lake air easy in my lungs. The night was a puzzle with its pieces all in place.

I sat next to Calla with our legs dangling. The other docks were visible around the edges of the lake. Tall trees filled the spaces between the houses on the other side of the water. The wind was calm, the moon a thumbnail sliver in the sky.

"If I tell you something, do you promise not to repeat it?" Calla asked. Her eyes were fixed straight ahead.

"Of course."

I think Big Sister secrets are one of the most important kinds.

Calla turned toward me, a huge grin on her face.

"Robby kissed me." Her voice sounded full, like she really wanted to scream it.

I gasped. Which instantly felt like the most uncool reaction I could have.

"When?" I asked, trying to redeem myself, even though I really wanted to ask ON THE LIPS?!

"Today after school. My friends have been telling me to do it ever since we started going out. But there's no time line for that kind of thing."

I'd heard girls on my team talk about kissing as "first base." Things seemed to get scarier the farther you got around the diamond. It made me want to just hide in the dugout forever.

"Was it . . . nice?"

Calla beamed at me, as bright as the stars, and nodded.

"Brooke, I know you just turned nine, and you're probably

not thinking about kissing anybody. But it's my sisterly duty to tell you to wait until you're ready. Wait until it's the most special thing you can think of."

Gus pulled into the driveway, the sound of his engine interrupting us. Dad stepped out with two white pizza boxes. Through the window I could see Mom leap off the couch to greet him. She appeared in the driveway a second later, wrapped her arms around his neck, stole one of the boxes.

The most special thing I could think of at that moment was this warm September night. So I told myself I would listen to Calla and wait for a moment that felt exactly like this.

CHAPTER NINE

A DISCOVERY

Derek and I watch the Orioles game in the TV room, on the lower level of our split-apart house. The room is painted forest green to match the big, squishy couch. Baseball caps and framed newspaper clippings cover the walls, and little figurines hang in boxes that have never been opened. I sit on the couch, and Derek sits on the floor in front of me, his head near my knee. The house is quiet, aside from the announcers on TV.

"This is not going well," Derek says. The Orioles are down by five in the sixth inning.

"There's still time," I say.

"But you have to factor in that it's the *Orioles*." Another Oriole strikes out, and Derek shakes his head. He's not wrong. They have been on a bit of a losing streak. For the past few years.

"Don't let my dad hear you say that."

"Good thing he's not here," he says. My heart flips over, thinking of how alone we are in the house.

I spring off the couch and walk over to the floor-to-ceiling bookshelf. The middle row has all our sports movies. *Remember the Titans, Rudy, The Sandlot.* Mom's favorite was *Cool Runnings,* and she would quote the whole thing as we watched. None of us stopped her. I haven't watched it in a long time. I'm afraid of what the movie will sound like without her narrating next to me.

Derek slides on his knees over to where I'm standing, and reaches into the bottom shelf. He pulls out a thick brown photo album.

"All the times I've been down here, I don't think I've ever looked at this." The cover of the album has a camera etched into the leather. Derek opens it.

"Wait," I blurt. He looks up at me, his brown eyes all confused.

"What?"

"I don't know if I . . ." The first page has only one picture: Dad, Mom, Calla, and me at our first baseball game as a family. Calla and I have orange foam fingers and plastic sunglasses, mine shaped like stars and hers like hearts.

Derek moves the album so I can't see it anymore.

"Too hard to look?"

I sit cross-legged on the carpet and take a breath.

"We'll find out."

Derek flips the book around so I can see it. There's a picture of little Calla crying in the flowers on the junior baseball field. A white ball sits next to her like a friend.

"Oh my gosh, it's her first day of T-ball! She tried to save the ball. I didn't know there was photo evidence."

"She does not look happy." Derek laughs.

"It just wasn't for her."

I look around the room. We're surrounded by sports, by my and Mom's and Dad's favorite things. I wonder if that's why Calla doesn't spend much time down here. None of this memorabilia represents her. No seed packets posted on the wall, no dried flowers pressed into a frame.

"What happened there?" Derek asks.

He's pointing to a picture of me at the kitchen table. I'm holding a bag of frozen peas to the side of my face. If I think hard, I can remember being in that exact moment, the bag numbing my cheek. Mom told me to look at the camera and say "peas."

"I was practicing fly balls with Dad and the sun got in my eyes. Mom decided practice was over."

Derek laughs again. He looks at me like he has something to say, but doesn't speak, and then turns the page to a set of pictures of a big, crowded picnic. I recognize the docks and the water, the bright green stretch of yard. It's Lincoln Lake. I look at a picture of my parents under a white banner that says LAKEFEST in blue lettering.

"Lakefest!" Derek reads. "How did I forget about Lakefest?"

There are pictures of kayak races, stacks of Papa Margherita's pizzas, a flower stand from Poppyseed Garden Center selling carnations for a dollar. It seems like everyone in town is there, and all the well-known businesses. I recognize Coach Tanaka, Mr. Spitz, Mom's friends from her job at the real estate office. Someone snapped a candid photo of Derek and me eating hot dogs in the grass, wrapped in striped towels.

"Lakefest," I say. The last Lakefest I can remember was when I was in fourth grade. "Those were really fun, weren't they?"

"They were the best." He touches a picture of himself and his abuela at a picnic table. She's jabbing at the corner of his mouth with a napkin.

The jingle of keys comes from upstairs, then the sound of Dad's footsteps. I pick up the album and take it with me to the landing.

"Orioles winning?" Dad asks, kicking off his shoes.

"Of course not," I answer. I turn the album to show him. "Dad, why don't we have Lakefest anymore?"

Dad squints down. His eyes fall on a photo of Mom in the middle of Hula-Hooping.

"Lakefest, huh. Haven't thought about that for a long time." He walks up the stairs and leaves his toolbox at the top. He's been at Fireplace House fixing a faucet. I follow him. Derek is behind me in the small stairwell.

"But why did it stop?" I ask.

Dad walks to the fridge and opens it. The bright light emphasizes how empty it is inside.

"It was a lot of work. Arranging vendors, doing the advertising." He closes the door. "And once we started renting to out-of-towners, it was harder to use all the yards at once. Your mom would have loved to keep it going, but it just didn't make sense anymore."

"I bet the renters would be okay with it. It's a party," Derek says. He goes to the living room and turns the Orioles game on.

"Yeah, and they were so much—" I start.

"Sorry, you two. But I don't even want to think about the houses right now." He opens the fridge door again like he's done some magic trick that made food appear. "Twenty-three needs a real plumber, and the cleaning fee from the group who destroyed twenty-five hasn't come through."

I clamp my lips together. A deep-voiced game announcer

says the Orioles are down by five. Dad groans and slams the fridge door. I lock eyes with Derek on the couch. We nod in a silent agreement to shut up about Lakefest. *For now.*

The front door opens and Calla steps in with a brown paper bag in her hands.

"Hey! Sorry I'm late. We needed groceries." She comes up the stairs and unloads the bag on the counter. Microwave rice, chocolate chip cookies, a loaf of bread. One of those precooked rotisserie chickens in a steamy plastic box.

"I would have stopped at the store, Cal." Dad reaches to help empty the bag, but Calla's already finished.

"It's fine, Dad."

She takes forks and plates out of the cabinet, and we all eat rotisserie chicken sandwiches to the sound of the Orioles losing.

That night, I slip the photo album under my pillow. I dream of balloons and kayaks and the lake. People are all spread out on the lawn, and twinkly white lights make the trees glow. The sun is setting, but no one wants to leave. I wake up breathless, wishing it were real.

CHAPTER TEN

BY THE LOCKERS

In science on Friday, Mrs. Valencia gives us the whole period to work on our projects. Aimi, Kasey, and Larissa wish me luck before I leave our corner. But I don't think I need it. It might have been Marley down on the dock the other day, and if it was, I shouldn't be afraid of her. Because I like to sit out there too, long enough for the world to go soft and quiet, until nothing exists but the lake and me.

I settle into the desk behind Marley. She flips her chair around to face me.

"Did you print those fact sheets?" She holds her hand out like there's no doubt I have them.

Luckily, I do.

"Yep." I give her the sheets from my binder. I reminded myself a thousand times to print the cockroach facts, and on reminder a thousand and one, I finally got off the couch and printed them.

I know it's a small task, but it felt like an accomplishment.

Marley flips through the papers, nods once, and hands them back to me. Her bangs are pinned to the side with little clips. I've always thought her eyes were brown, but I notice now that they're dark green.

"Great." She unfolds our cardboard poster on her desk. I see the pencil squares she drew last class to show where we (she) want to put things. She's added some flower stickers in the blank spaces. "Thanks for doing that. I would have, but I don't have a printer right now."

"Because you're staying at the lake house?"

It slips out before I can stop myself. Marley's eyes turn to green venom.

"Who told you that?" She flattens her palm on the poster board, smudges a pencil line.

"No one," I lie. "I thought I saw you. On the dock. My family rents those houses out, so I was just . . . there."

I don't dare ask about her mom and the chain saw and the tooth. I'm scared to even *think* about it right now, with Marley glaring at me like she wants to spike a volleyball at my face. I look around the class. Kasey, Aimi, and Larissa are laughing in their corner. Mrs. Valencia let them work as a group of three on the insect project. Other partners work side by side at their desks. No one notices me in peril over here.

"Then you know it's just temporary," she says. "We're only staying for two more weeks."

"Yeah. Of course. Sorry, I shouldn't have said anything."

Marley takes a breath in, exhales for what feels like an hour. She grabs a pencil and fixes the line she smudged.

"All right. We have paragraphs about eating habits, life cycle, mating behavior. I want to do more research on their environment and anatomy. And then we have to start working on our speech. Do you think you can do that?"

My head spins. She's listed so many tasks, I can barely tell which one is mine, what she actually wants me to do. I need a second to let it sink in. When I don't respond, she lifts her eyes from the poster.

"Brooke?" she asks.

The surprise of her saying my name snaps me out of my spiral. It feels like taking a step from strangers to acquaintances.

"Yeah, sorry. Can you say that again?"

"The speech part. Will you start putting that together?"

It's more responsibility than she's given me so far on this project. Is she starting to trust me?

"Yeah, I can come up with some stuff." I add the assignment to my list of mental reminders and hope it sticks.

Marley stares at me an extra second.

"What's your organization style?" she asks. She takes a sticker book and blue scissors out of her backpack.

"Wait, what? Is that a cockroach thing?"

"No, it has nothing to do with bugs. Do you use a planner? Voice recording?"

I imagine listening to my to-do list like Calla's podcast. *Welcome to My Mess*, the host would announce.

"Neither. Nothing. I just keep it all in my head," I tell her. She nods like it's the answer she was expecting.

"The brain isn't always the best storage system," Marley says. She slaps a glittery letter *C* sticker onto the poster, then an *O*. "That's what Organizer Olivia says."

"Who?" I pick up the sticker book, pull out another *C*, and hand it to her. She glances at me before peeling it off my finger and pasting it down.

"She posts videos and blogs about how to keep track of things. Some of it's pretty simple, but it's really helpful. The organization styles are active, creative, and direct."

"Interesting," I say. I don't think I fall into any of those categories. I hand her the *K* and *R*.

"Take out your notebook," Marley says.

I follow her order. If I had to guess, I'd say Marley is the direct type.

"What do you have to do right now?" she asks. "Like, what chores and homework and stuff."

I think about that list. It feels like being clobbered by a baseball bat.

"I have a paper for English, two worksheets for math, dishes I told my sister I'd put away when I get home, laundry on the floor, a softball game tomorrow." I count the tasks off on my fingers.

"And starting on our speech," she reminds me, opening her own notebook.

"Right." In my head, I add more to the list. *Wonder and worry about Calla's broken heart. Keep Dad happy while he's drowning in work. Deal with stomach flutters from Derek. Miss Mom every second.*

"The most basic tool you can use is a to-do list. Write each task on its own line, and then draw a box in front of it that you can check off when you finish." She flips her notebook around. Her to-do list is written down the page. Some of her boxes are crossed out with a purple *X*.

    ☒ Read two chapters for English.
    ☒ Practice flute.
    ☐ Dinner with Dad.
    ☐ Family therapy.

I start writing my list before she catches me staring at hers. Maybe what Lily said about Marley's parents was true. When I finally look up, Marley's eyes are shining in a totally different way than before. She bites her bottom lip like she's fighting a smile.

"Yeah, good job. It's really helped me. You can even put a sticker on the boxes instead of a check mark, but that's more of a creative-type thing." Her words come out quick, like she has a lot to get out and this is her only chance.

"Thank you," I say, and mean it. A weird burst of excitement stirs in my stomach. It's like the list makes me want to do the work so I can check off the little boxes.

We turn back to our project. Marley tells me what to do, as usual, but her voice is less sharp than before. Half an hour later, Mrs. Valencia tells us to clean up our supplies.

"Parting is such sweet sorrow," Mrs. Valencia says, pretending to wipe a tear away.

Marley tucks the poster under her arm.

"I have some of Organizer Olivia's blogs printed out in my locker. Do you want them?" she asks.

I keep my notebook open to the to-do list so I won't forget, and jam it into my binder.

"Definitely," I answer. I like the idea of holding something in my hands that will tell me exactly what to do. Like a map to being a better Brooke.

The bell rings, and Kasey waves at me from the corner. I shake my head. Aimi draws a question mark in the air, and Larissa laughs. I try not to feel jealous that the three of them get to be a group for the project. Working with Marley isn't so bad. When it's not nerve-racking, it's actually pretty educational.

Our lockers are halfway down the hall. I follow Marley's ruby-colored backpack through the crowds getting out of class. Loud laughing overpowers all the other sounds. It's the cackling, witchy kind of laughter that only comes from making fun of someone. Lily stands to the side of the hall with three of her friends. Their heads are close together, and their eyes are on Marley. My stomach flips over.

"Are you coming?" Marley asks, looking over her shoulder.

I nod. It feels like my sneakers are full of rocks. I stand next to Marley at locker number seventy-two, twirl my lock while she twirls hers. My hands are so shaky, I dial the wrong combination and have to try again. Marley's locker opens. A white page falls to the floor like a failed paper airplane. She picks it up and unfolds it; I'm close enough to see a cartoony picture drawn in red marker. It's a giant tooth with a bubble caption: *Stay away from Bossy Floss.*

Marley holds the drawing with two hands. She stares at it long enough for people passing by to look over her shoulder, laugh at the tooth, and walk away. I turn around and catch Lily's eye. She shrugs at me. The overhead lights shine off her hair so brightly, it's like she's wearing a gold crown. She bounces off with her group.

"Marley?" I step closer, but carefully, like Dad when he's taking down a hornet's nest.

She tears the drawing in half.

"I'm sorry," I say.

"You didn't do anything." Her voice is sharp. Maybe I didn't put the drawing in her locker, but I do owe Marley an apology. I've called her Bossy Floss before without thinking how much it must sting. She reaches for the top shelf of her locker and pulls out a checkered folder. "Here."

She hands it to me. The label on the front says *Organizer Olivia Blogs*. I have to blink a few times, because I forgot what Marley was going into her locker for in the first place. She shoves the pieces of the drawing into her pocket, makes them disappear. It's almost like the drawing never happened.

It reminds me of Calla.

Everything suddenly feels heavy. Marley's to-do list, the rumors about her parents, Dad looking into the empty refrigerator. Calla without Robby. Mom being gone. I finally get my locker open and squeeze the folder between two textbooks. The fuzzy photo at the lake tugs at my attention. I squint, try to make our faces clearer, try to force the world to make sense. The background is so hard to decipher, but suddenly, like lightning, I notice something I haven't before: a Lakefest sign in the trees behind us. The photo must have been taken at the first-ever Lakefest.

A plan swirls around in my head. A big plan. The biggest plan.

What if there's a way to bring back the past? A sunshiny, perfect time, like the one in this photo? There's no way I can pull it off alone. But now I know someone good enough at organizing to help me make it happen.

And someone who might need sunshine just as much as I do.

"Do you want to help me bring back a town picnic?" I ask.

Marley keeps her eyes on the floor. Anticipation squeezes me in a bear hug. Every possible response she could give me (*yes, no, go away and never talk to me again*) has run through my head by the time she finally looks up.

"Okay."

CHAPTER ELEVEN

BACON BEANS

I'm on my bed texting Derek between math problems. His abuela found her hearing aid, but now her dentures are missing. Derek's description of her toothless speech is gross but funny, and makes me wish he were here to tell the story in person.

The air fills with a thick smell. Something like brown sugar and smoke. I get out of bed and walk to the kitchen, where Calla stands at the stove, her hair in a fluffy bronze bun. The pan in front of her sizzles and steams.

"Dinner's just about done. Come set the table, please." She waves a wooden spoon. My heart shrivels at the stress in her voice. We used to have sword fights with utensils while we set the table together, back when Calla only helped Mom with the cooking and wasn't totally responsible for dinner existing at all. Our last duel feels like a lifetime ago.

I go to the cabinet, studying her frying pan.

"What is it?" I ask.

"It's baked beans with bacon mixed in. I call them Bacon Beans."

Calla stirs the bubbling brown liquid. The white stovetop is streaked with her muddy creation.

"Looks . . . brown," I say.

She rolls her eyes. "I know, IdidwhatIcouldwithwhatwehave, but it'll taste better than it looks."

Her complaint zips by. But it's true. Dad grocery shops like the house is a concession stand. Lots of hot dogs and frozen fries. We order takeout from Papa Margherita's at least twice a week. He's too busy working to think about what ingredients go together.

"I'm sure it will," I say, and open the utensil drawer in front of me. "Do we use forks or spoons for Bacon Beans?"

She half laughs. "Let's go with spoons."

Dad gets home a few minutes later. Calla pours the Bacon Beans into a serving dish and brings it to the table with orange oven mitts. I follow with three bowls.

"How are my girls today?" Dad asks. He hangs his black jacket on the banister.

"Pretty good," Calla says. "But student council went long, so I feel like a zombie."

"Uh-oh. Don't go eating our brains." Dad zombie-groans the word "brains."

Calla *ewws* and I giggle. I think Dad is the funniest person in the world. He can send Derek and me into fits of laughter with one facial expression. The jokes didn't go away after Mom's accident, but they're different. They remind me of the hollow thud that comes from knocking on wood. An empty sound.

We sit at the table and take sloppy scoops of the Bacon Beans. I swallow a fast bite. Calla was right. It does taste better than it looks. It's hot and comforting, like soup on a sick day.

"This is awesome. Salty meets sweet perfection," Dad says with his mouth full.

I nod in agreement. Calla smiles and takes her first bite.

"If I've learned anything in cooking club, it's that seasoning is key," she says.

Dad blows a raspberry. "I don't know, Cal. Student council, cooking club, your schoolwork . . ." He puts his hand on the table, close to Calla's. "You don't want to burn yourself out."

Calla prickles. She shifts away from his hand.

"It's junior year. I have to push myself," she says.

Dad nods and takes his hand back. Like me, he's heard

the junior year speech before. I wonder if the idea of Calla leaving us for college scares him as much as it scares me.

"I just want to make sure you have time to be a kid. Spend time with your friends and Robby."

I choke on a boiling-hot bite of Bacon Beans. It burns the roof of my mouth. Calla shoots me a look that Dad sees.

"Did I miss something?" he asks.

The burnt spot in my mouth throbs to the rhythm of my heartbeat. He doesn't know about the breakup.

"Robby and I . . ."

Dad reaches out again. This time he squeezes Calla's shoulder.

"It's okay, Cal. You don't have to say it. That's a hard thing."

My mouth-heartbeat continues pounding. I wish Calla *would* say it. But not all fast and sandwiched between other words. I want her to say how she feels, explain why she broke up with Robby in the first place. Calla swirls a spoon around in her bowl; her fern-green eyes look like Marley's when she unfolded that drawing at her locker.

It's time for my brilliant Lakefest plan to start working its magic.

"I came up with an idea," I say. Dad and Calla turn to me. Calla looks relieved that I changed the subject. "I want to bring back Lakefest. Well, I want *us* to bring it back. As a family."

I wait for a slow smile to spread across Dad's face as he realizes this is exactly what everyone needs. Calla will start rattling off ideas, and I'll rush to find a notebook to write them all down in.

Instead, squiggly lines appear in Dad's forehead. Calla's lips press tight together.

"Lakefest is a lot of work," Dad says. "Your mom and I put hours into planning those events. I don't have that time right now." He wipes his glasses. They're fogged up from the steaming bowl.

"It's a nice thought, but I can't really work on it with you either." Calla tips her spoon, lets the bean sauce drip back into her bowl.

"A girl from school, Marley, can help me. She's staying in Skylight House right now. And I know Derek will help too. We can all split up the work. We can do it." I sound like I'm begging.

Dad takes a bite and chews for way too long.

"I actually wanted to talk to you both about the houses." Dad's eyes are cast down at the table. It's not the kind of look that comes before good news. "I'm thinking about selling them."

I slam down my spoon. "WHAT?"

I've heard about people's lives flashing before their eyes. That happens to me now with my life at the lake: All the days I've spent there. Mega Float. I watch the memories fade.

"Brooke." Calla shakes her head at me.

How can she have nothing to say? Her face is as blank as a brick wall. I want to cry into my bowl of Bacon Beans. Or smash it.

"It's hard to keep up with them by myself. This would be a good thing for us." Dad rubs his eyes.

"I can help more. I can do whatever it takes, Dad. Please don't give them up." I need the houses. My lungs clog from just the thought of not having my easy-breathing place anymore.

"Nothing is set in stone. Try to keep an open mind."

"Can I be excused?" I ask.

I dash down the hall to my room before Dad answers. I step over dirty clothes to curl up in a ball on my bed. The photo album under my pillow is a lump against my cheek. We can't have Lakefest if the houses aren't ours. It feels like my plan is over before it even started.

CHAPTER TWELVE

THE MEANING OF A KNEE BUMP

Derek lives in a duplex apartment with his mom, Doris, and his abuela, on the same street as the fire department. The spontaneous sirens always scare me, like it's a signal for an alien invasion. Derek can sleep right through them. We're eating sliced fruit at his kitchen table on Saturday morning. Both of us play at noon today. Dad is meeting the plumber at Fireplace House, and Calla has a car wash for Spanish club, so Doris is bringing me to the game.

I pulverize a strawberry with my fork. I had a dream about Lakefest last night, and it's stuck in my head. The sky was gray and no one came. I sat under a torn banner by myself.

Derek clears his throat.

"I think you won," he says, motioning to the strawberry massacre on my plate.

I laugh and take a bite. Derek's jokes are the perfect distraction. That, and the fact that his leg is close to mine under the table, and makes contact every once in a while.

"Let's hope we're both saying that after our games," I answer.

He pops a grape into his mouth. "Is there a reason you're murdering fruit?"

Another knee bump. Another flash of heat in my cheeks.

"I want to bring Lakefest back," I admit. "I told Dad and Calla about it, but they said I shouldn't bother."

I wait for his reaction. What if he agrees with them? He finishes chewing. His face doesn't give anything away.

"Let's still do it," he finally says.

My heart breaks out in sunbeams. It's not just that he likes the idea; it's that he automatically put himself on my team. No questions asked.

"Are you sure? My dad made it seem like it's a lot of work. I don't think we ever knew that because we just got to go and have fun."

"We'll still get to go and have fun."

His words push my doubts away. *We're really doing this.*

"You're the absolute best, D," I tell him. "And it won't be all on us. Marley Macintosh said she would help too."

Derek's face clouds up. He clears our plates and drops

them into the sink. The number twenty-five is printed on the back of his red jersey, the same number as Flamingo House. I wonder if he still thinks about what almost happened in the flamingo room.

"Marley? Really?" he asks with his back still toward me.

His tone fills my stomach with sharp nerves.

"She seems really good with organization and stuff," I tell him.

When he finally turns around, his expression lands somewhere between cold and confused.

"I didn't think you talked to her," he says.

"I don't really. But we're doing that cockroach project together in science."

"And Lakefest came up?"

The excitement I felt earlier fades. Did I make a mistake by inviting Marley to join me?

"Lily had just done something mean to her. She put a drawing in Marley's locker that said 'Bossy Floss.' I felt bad, so I asked her to help."

Derek's face warms a little, but not completely.

"Isn't she, like . . . not nice?" he asks. "I mean, people call her that name for a reason."

A rush of frustration makes me curl my hands into fists. I wish I had another strawberry to stab.

"*Lily's* the one who's not *nice.*"

"Yeah, but people actually like her."

His words leave me speechless. I didn't know Derek was capable of saying something so hurtful, so Lily-like. His eyes widen and he rushes back to his seat, like he sees the mess he made and needs to fix it. His knee full-on crashes into mine when he sits.

"I shouldn't have said that. I bet you made Marley feel better, and it sounds like we need all the help we can get."

I smile at him, even though what he said still rings in my ears.

"It's going to be so great, D. Just like old times."

He doesn't move his knee away, not until ten minutes later, when Doris comes into the kitchen and says it's time to go.

CHAPTER THIRTEEN

CURVEBALLS

Our game is against the Swirly-Q Ice Cream Crushers. They're the last-place team in the league. If we win, we're officially in the championship tournament, but Mom always said not to pay attention to things like standings. *Don't rub it in when you're better, don't argue when you're worse,* she'd say. *That's what being a good sport is.* I hand Coach Tanaka the forged form before the game, trying to ignore the sinking feeling in the pit of my stomach.

I squat into position as a Crusher comes up to bat. A catcher has a lot to keep track of—calling pitches, positioning your glove, checking for runners stealing second base. Not to mention the bat swinging full speed above your head. But behind the plate, I'm in control. I know what to do and how to do it.

The batter's jersey has the white outline of a soft-serve

ice cream cone on the front and the number eight on the back. I don't know her name, but I think she's in the grade under me. Blond hair spills out of her helmet.

Lily waits on the mound for me to give her a signal. I wave my hand in the sign not to do a special pitch. We're winning seven to zero in the fourth inning, so there's no need for anything fancy. Lily winds up, and the ball zips, rocket fast, toward the outside corner of home plate. At the last minute, it curls in hard, and the batter swings. The curveball punches into my palm.

"Strike one," the umpire says.

I'm glad Lily can't see me glare from behind my mask. Throwing me an unexpected pitch could easily end in disaster. If the ball gets past me and I have to scramble for it, it gives the other team the chance to steal a base. Not to mention I could get hurt. But Lily doesn't seem to care about anyone. Not the Crushers, not me. Not Marley. Maybe it's time Lily gets thrown a curveball.

"Wait to swing," I whisper to number eight.

"What?" she asks. I see a temporary tattoo of an ice cream cone on her cheek.

"She's going to throw a changeup." I hold out my mitt. "Trust me."

She turns to get into her batting stance. I circle my finger in the changeup signal. Lily nods, her visor casting shadows over her perfect face. She pitches again. The ball comes slowly this time. I take my eyes off it for a second, the number one no-no of being a catcher, to glance at the batter. She keeps her arms back, waiting for the ball, until it finally crosses the plate. Her swing connects, and the hit shoots through Aimi's legs at second base. Number eight sprints to first. She makes it there easily before our right fielder can throw the ball in. Lily kicks the pitcher's mound with her pink cleat.

I don't think sabotaging my own teammate makes me a good sport. But maybe standing up for Marley does? I look at the sky and hope the softball gods, and Mom, forgive me.

Two innings later, the game ends ten to three. My team forms a huddle to celebrate making it to the championship tournament. Our lion roar echoes through the whole athletic complex. Dad, who made it to the game around the fifth inning, claps hard on the bleachers with the other parents.

Coach Tanaka dismisses us to pack our gear. I sit on the bucket in my Disaster Corner, unstrapping my shin guards. Lily storms over to me with her hands curled into fists.

"You give away pitches now?" she snaps. Her cheeks are rosy red.

Lily's queen bee powers sting me until my wings go weak. I know why I gave number eight the pitch. But now it seems like the worst idea in the world.

"What do you mean?" I ask.

"Don't be stupid." She crosses her arms. "I just heard that you told Leigh Kennedy how to swing for the changeup. Is this because of what happened with your new BFF?"

I'm not sure Marley is even the *friend* part of BFF. But ever since I saw her sitting on that dock, ever since she told me there are organization styles, I've wanted to know more about her than what people say.

"I don't get why you would draw that and put it in her locker," I admit.

Lily rolls her ice-blue eyes. "It's not like it was aimed at you. You just happened to be there." She scans me up and down, and I go into self-conscious mode. "You're fine. You're . . . cool."

I don't want her words to feel so sparkly special. What she did to Marley was wrong. But it feels essential to be on Lily's good side. Otherwise, it could be my locker stuffed with awful drawings.

It makes sense that Derek was so hesitant to work on Lakefest with Marley, when she has an enemy as powerful as Lily. But I wish it didn't.

"I'm sorry for spoiling the pitch. It won't happen again. Promise."

Lily nods like her work here is done. She turns on her heel and flies away.

I peel off one shin guard and then the other, slowly, and put them into my bat bag without shaking off the dirt.

CHAPTER FOURTEEN
FOUND iN THE SPAM FOLDER

Dad drives us home, dropping Derek off on the way. Dad's quiet, so quiet that I wonder if he heard about my sabotage. I try making jokes about Gus and singing to the radio in a ridiculous voice, but he doesn't laugh. My breaths are unsteady when we finally pull into the driveway. I lunge for the door, ready to grab my bag from the truck bed and rush inside before he can say—

"Hold on, Brooke. I found something in my spam folder today."

Dad takes his phone out of the cupholder. I watch him open his email inbox. Two emails from Carrie Valencia sit at the top of the list. My stomach goes full-blown pretzel.

"I can explain," I say, even though I can't. I didn't tell him about Mrs. Valencia's email, and there's no explanation.

"'Dear Mr. Dell, I hope you are well,'" Dad reads. "'I am writing to notify you that Brooke, while a pleasure to have in class, seems to have a hard time remembering her homework assignments. It's my policy to reach out to the parents after a third missed assignment, which Brooke just reached.'"

"Dad," I try to interrupt. He holds up his hand.

"'I have let Brooke know that I would be sending this email, and that you should respond so we can come up with a solution to help Brooke complete her work. I look forward to hearing from you. Carrie Valencia.'"

I don't say anything. Silence stews between us like a pan of Bacon Beans.

"Should I read the follow-up email she sent when I didn't respond to the first?" he asks.

"No, thank you."

Dad leans back on the headrest with his eyes closed.

"It's my fault," he says. "I haven't had time to help you stay on track. Your mom was so good at that. But you're a little scatterbrained, like me. We let things slip."

It's dark in the car, but even this shadowy version of Dad looks exhausted. I want to cry and hug him and take away every bit of weight that I've piled onto his shoulders.

"I'm so sorry, Dad. I promise I'm going to be better with my work. I'm going to learn about all these new organization tips a friend in class told me about, and this will never happen again."

Dad's head rolls to the side. His eyes are serious and hold mine.

"It's okay to make mistakes, Brookie. But don't keep them to yourself. I won't be mad if you just tell me the truth."

The forged emergency form comes storming into my thoughts. I should come clean right now. But the confession stays lodged in my throat. *I won't do anything like that again. I won't. He doesn't need to know.*

"Okay, Dad."

Dad twists the key out of the ignition. Gus's inside lights flicker on.

"We're going to help each other. You, me, and Calla. We're a team," he says. He gets out of the truck and grabs my bag for me, then takes it to the basement through the side door of the house.

I stay in the truck for an extra second, feeling like the slimy scum on the bottom of Lincoln Lake.

Error #1

Before the concession stand became the Madeline Dell Memorial Concession Stand, Mom would get there early, hours ahead of the first games each Saturday. Sometimes I'd stay home with Dad until game time, and he and Calla and I would drive to the fields together in Gus. Other times, I'd go early with her to help set up the stand. The soft sunlight would cover the empty parking lot, and it was just me and Mom and all those baseball diamonds.

It was one of the early-with-Mom mornings on the day of my semifinal game. We'd just finished opening the concession stand. Greasy hot dogs spun around on the roller, and the candy rack was fully restocked. A perfect Softball Saturday.

"Ready for the rush?" Mom asked. She tore the plastic packaging from a case of blue Gatorade.

I looked out the window. Two senior boys stood a few feet away. They had their hats on backward.

"I think I can handle it." I threw Mom a thumbs-up, and she did one back.

The boys stepped up to the window. The one with thick black eyebrows and a faint mustache cleared his throat.

"Can we get, uh, two blue slushies," he said.

"Mix mine," the other chimed in. He had freckles on every inch of his face. "Red and blue."

"Wait, mine too. And shake it."

"I can't shake it," I answered, imagining the slushie spilling out of the lid. Slushie lids aren't known for their stability.

The boys laughed, but I hadn't meant to be funny.

"Wouldn't want to see you try," the freckly one said to the other, almost too quiet for me to hear. Definitely too quiet for Mom to hear by the fridge. I turned toward her, but she didn't look back.

The slushie mix tumbled in frosty circles when I pulled the handles to fill the cups, first with red then blue. The colors blended into each other. I focused on the cold to put out the fire spreading across my face. I didn't even know these boys, but it was like they knew me. Like they'd studied just how to make my body burn up.

I passed the slushies to them through the window.

"Two red-and-blue slushies," I said.

Almost-Mustache slapped a five-dollar bill onto the counter. Freckles puckered his lips before he walked away. I *forgot I was at the fields. I forgot I loved this place. In that moment, I wanted to be anywhere else.*

"I'm taking the trash out," I told Mom.

"What? Sweetie, there's nothing in it."

I looked down into the trash can. It seemed like a good place to hide. The only garbage inside was the Gatorade packaging.

"There's wrappings."

I tugged the black bag out of the can and tied the plastic handles into a bow. The bag flew out, as light as air, and Mom narrowed her eyes.

"All right, silly," she said. She shut the foggy door of the fridge. I left out the back with the garbage bag.

The boys were there at a picnic table, facing away from me. I walked slowly, careful not to disturb the rocks on the path to the garbage can, careful that my sandals didn't slap against my heels and give my location away.

"That girl was rough," Freckles said. He took the lid off his slushie and tilted his head back, dumping the rest of the drink into his mouth.

"Yeah. A two out of ten."

The basically empty garbage bag felt heavy somehow. I dropped it onto the path and rushed back into the concession stand.

Mom's eyes flashed when she saw me.

"Spot a monster or something?" she asked.

I couldn't tell Mom what had happened. The thought of saying "I'm a two" out loud felt too embarrassing. Even worse, it felt true. It wasn't like I thought I was an amazingly beautiful specimen or anything. I knew I wasn't Lily. I just didn't want that to matter so much.

I didn't want two boys in backward hats to make it matter.

Mom didn't push me when I said I was nervous for the game. I reorganized the candy racks until Larissa's mom and Kasey's dad, the other parents working the concession stand that day, showed up.

In the third inning of my game, the same boys passed by the junior softball field. One side of my brain said, Focus, *there's a runner stealing second. The other side said,* Two out of ten.

The two-out-of-ten side won. My second-base throw was late and went straight over Aimi's head. Sophia ran in to try to save it in center field. But the runner had already made it to third.

I tried to tuck away the image of those swirled slushies, and the thoughts they put in my head. That I was ugly. That no boy could possibly like me.

But that overthrow was my first big mistake in softball. I can't forget it.

CHAPTER FIFTEEN
PAPA MARGHERITA'S

The next day is May first, and it comes with a pure kind of warmth that sticks around until evening. It reminds me that summer is rolling in. Soon the sun will stay up for hours longer, leaving more time to play catch in the yard. I call a Lakefest meeting with Derek at Papa Margherita's Pizza at five o'clock. We jog there from our houses once in a while, because it's good exercise, and because slices are only a dollar. My backpack bounces against my butt as I run. The photo album is inside.

Derek is sitting on a bench outside the little brick building. He looks up from his phone and grins.

"I win," he says.

"We've calculated this. My run is point-oh-three miles longer than yours."

"I'll give you a head start next time."

"Deal."

Derek holds the door for me. I'm immediately smacked with the familiar cheese-and-hot-pepper smell. The counter is covered with the same white boxes our garbage and fridge are usually filled with.

Papa Margherita himself (okay, his real name is Jensen) is at the register. He's wearing a black apron and burgundy cowboy boots. I've heard him tell Dad that his body may live near the lake, but his heart lives on a ranch in Texas.

"You order something, Thing Two?" Jensen flips through his little receipt book. I smile at the nickname. Calla is Thing One.

"We're eating in," I answer. "I'll have a slice of bacon and tomato, please."

"Broccoli and cheddar for me, thanks." Derek eyes the photos of Papa Margherita's baseball team by the beverage cooler. He's front row in three of them. I think Derek's team has the best sponsor in the league, but the Poppyseed Garden Center is a close second. Anything is better than the J&B Funeral Home.

Jensen nods. "Take a seat. Two slices coming up." He doesn't bother writing our order down.

The TV on the wall is playing a horse race. A few older men watch on stools at the counter with coffee mugs.

Sometimes I feel like everyone in Papa Margherita's has been here before. It's like a living room for the town.

A new wave of determination crashes over me: Lakefest will bring people together the way this place does. I grab Derek's hand and tug him toward the seating area. We're at our usual booth in the corner before I realize what I've done.

"Sorry," I say. I drop his hand like a dead fish.

"Don't be."

We slide quickly into either side of the booth. The tables are marbled gray Formica, with white paper place mats. I busy my hands and brain to stop thinking about the calluses on Derek's palm. I put the photo album between us.

"Is that the album from the TV room?" Derek asks. He takes off his red baseball cap and puts it on the bench next to him.

I flip past the pictures of Calla in the flowers and my frozen-pea incident to the Lakefest spread.

"I thought it might inspire us. I've been sleeping with it under my pillow." I pull a photo out of the album to look at it closer. It's a shot of middle-school-age Robby and another kid paddling yellow kayaks in the lake. Calla is mid-jump on the dock.

"Really, you have?" Derek tears the corner off a napkin and flicks it in my direction.

My face heats like I'm standing at the pizza oven. Was that embarrassing to admit? Well, too late to take it back now.

"It's been making me dream about Lakefest."

Derek smiles, and now it's like I'm *inside* the pizza oven.

"Is that stupid?" I ask.

"No. It's cool to know what you dream about."

I flick the piece of napkin back at him, because what other response is there when someone says something like that? Something that shows they care about what goes on in your brain. That maybe they even wonder about it. Over Derek's shoulder, I see Jensen heading toward us with a tray. The rest of the booths are empty except for one by the window. A man with dark hair in a blue suit is sitting across from a girl with the same dark hair. I can only see the back of her head. But it's become a familiar head: *Marley*.

"A bacon tomato, a broccoli cheddar, and cheesy bread on the house." Jensen gives us our slices on paper plates and puts the basket of bread in the middle of the table. It's steaming hot and smells like garlic.

"Wow, thanks, Jensen." Derek takes a piece. "Are you sure?"

"Get our team a championship, and we'll call it even." He leaves to drop a check at Marley's table. His boots clop on the floor as he heads back to the ovens.

"So what's step one?" Derek shakes Parmesan onto his broccoli-speckled slice.

"Of what?" A barely eaten pepperoni pizza sits between Marley and the man. He takes out his wallet and leaves a few bills on the table.

"Lakefest. Where do we start?"

Marley slides out of her booth. When she stands, she ends up looking straight at me.

"By assembling the team," I say. I wave her over. She hesitates, then taps the man on the shoulder and points toward our booth. Derek turns around to see who I'm talking to.

"Oh."

Marley and the man talk for a second, and then she rolls her eyes and starts walking over. The man follows. She stands next to our table like a waitress ready to take our order.

"Hi. This is my dad." She points to the man. "Dad, this is Brooke. We have science together. And this is Derek. He's in our grade too."

Mr. Macintosh grins. He has the straightest, whitest teeth I've ever seen. Dentist teeth, I guess. I can't help but think about Marley's to-do list from class. She can cross off *dinner with Dad* now.

"Nice to meet you both." He drops a business card and a twenty-dollar bill onto the table.

"Dad," Marley growls.

"What? I want to treat your friends to their dinner. Is that so bad?" He winks at Derek and me. "Five minutes, Marley. I'll wait in the car."

He walks away, and Marley takes a deep breath. The business card has *Gordon T. Macintosh, DDS* printed in blue letters, and under that it reads *What does your smile say about you?*

"You don't have to take that card. Or the money. He's trying to suck up to me," Marley says. She gets into the booth next to me before I can move over, and our hips collide. I scramble to the side.

"It's okay. We appreciate it." I pick up the card and slide it into the album like a photo. "Welcome to the first meeting of Team Lakefest."

I glance at Derek. He starts to roll the stray napkin crumb between his fingers. He doesn't look mad or mean, because Derek's face is never really mad or mean, but he doesn't look happy, either.

"Lakefest. Good name. Are those your references?" She motions toward the album.

"Yeah, these are pictures from the old picnics," Derek chimes in. He points to a photo of me and him in the grass.

"The last one was the summer of fourth grade," I tell her.

"We always had the best time," Derek says. "You never went, right?"

Marley wouldn't notice, but Derek's voice is stormy. I look at him like he's a stranger. Why is he acting like this?

"No. We moved to Lincoln two years ago, when my parents opened their office." She glares at her dad's card in the plastic pouch. "Looks like a lot of the businesses in town were there. That's great."

"I'm hoping the same places will want to be part of it again. The garden center, the kayak rental place, the food trucks."

Marley tilts her head, nods. "Cool. But we don't have to limit ourselves to what the picnic used to be. There are probably new or different places we could ask too. Do you have a date in mind?"

"May fifteenth," I say without thinking. Mom's birthday.

"You do know that's in only two weeks." Marley's eyebrows pop toward her bangs.

"I'm eager, I guess." Eager because Dad could decide to sell the houses any second. I need Lakefest to make him remember how much they mean to us before he does.

Outside, a black SUV flashes its headlights. Marley sighs.

"I have to go. But the pictures are helpful. We have a

lot to do. Talk to you guys soon?" She rushes out of the booth before we can answer.

I watch through the window as Marley climbs into her dad's car.

"Definitely bossy," Derek says. It makes me think of Lily's drawing, and my stomach turns.

"She's not so bad. I think she'll help us pull this off."

I smile at Derek as big as I can. He smiles back, but not in his normal way. Dr. Macintosh's business card sits in the album between us. What does this smile say about Derek?

CHAPTER SIXTEEN

VIOLETS

I go with Calla to the garden center on Monday. On the way, she tells me about a grease fire in cooking club and an argument in student council over the DJ for the spring dance. I soak up her words like a sponge. If I can only have Calla in bits and pieces, I'll savor this storytelling moment in her car with the windows down, sister to sister.

"I'm so glad Spanish club got canceled today," she says. "I need some plant therapy." She turns into the Poppyseed parking lot. The lot barely has any spaces because it's packed with bags of soil, rows of flowers, and pots big enough for me to fit in. We park in the back corner by the greenhouse.

Poppyseed smells like the day after a big storm. Wind chimes sing when we walk in, making it feel like we've entered a fantasy world where flowers reach down from hanging pots like enchanted vines.

"What are you looking for?" I ask.

"Violets," she says. "The garden could use some color."

There's almost no one in the greenhouse, so we can stop and look at as many plants as we want without getting in anyone's way. The violets are on the other side of the room. We pass a table of garden gnomes and some wooden crates with flowers wrapped in parchment paper. They look like the bouquets that Poppyseed used to sell at Lakefest.

"Do you think Dad will really sell the houses?" I ask.

Calla pauses by a wire shelf of herbs. She picks up a basil pot and studies it, the fresh scent wafting off the leaves.

"I'm not sure. It probably wouldn't be the worst thing."

I stare at a scallion sprout and try to make sense of her words. It would one hundred percent be the worst thing. Memories of Mom are woven into those houses like a tapestry.

"But they're *ours*."

I realize that I sound bratty. But does Calla really not care? I'm tired of my sister being a mystery to me; it wasn't like this when Mom was here. Last December, after the first big snowstorm of the winter, Calla and I were clearing the sidewalk at the empty Purple Couch House when she dropped her shovel to the ground and screamed up at the dull gray sky. I stood frozen in my snow boots with no clue what to say; she picked up her shovel and apologized before I could ask what had happened.

"Think about it seriously, Brookie," she says now. She puts the basil down and starts walking. "I'm going to be leaving for college in a year. You'll have your own things going on. Dad won't have enough help. And hiring an assistant is expensive."

"I'll never be too busy for him." I think part of me is accusing her, *Not like you being too busy for us.*

We're at the violets now. Calla picks out one of the biggest bunches and sighs into the petals. It looks like she has a purple beard.

"You say that now. We've had a lot of good times there, of course, but sometimes you just have to be logical and move on."

I want to tell her that it's the good times that are going to fix everything, not logic. Trying to "move on" has me messing up on the field, Calla dumping her boyfriend, and Dad selling our precious places on the lake. Mom wouldn't approve of any of this.

"I guess," I say instead. I don't need Calla raining all over my Lakefest parade right now.

She tucks a plastic pot of violets into the crook of each elbow and heads for the register. I follow. From behind, it looks like the flowers are growing out of her body.

Yohanna, my favorite Poppyseed cashier, is behind the counter. She's in her twenties and has orange dreadlocks. I notice that her hands are streaked with soil when she scans the barcodes on the pots.

"Haven't seen you in a bit," she says. She has a gap between her front teeth that makes some of her words whistle.

"Junior year is a monster." Calla plucks a cucumber seed packet from the display next to the register. She sounds like a robot with a programmed response for why she's stopped doing the things she used to. *Junior year. Boop. So busy. Beep.*

"How's the team doing, Brooke?" Yohanna asks while she scans the seeds.

"On our way to another trophy," I answer.

I look at the Lions photos behind her, like the ones in Papa Margherita's. Three different Brookes look back at me: ten-year-old me with sun in her eyes, eleven-year-old me with a bad haircut, this-year me with my catcher's gear on.

"Super."

Calla hands over her Garden Pass, and four dollars is taken off the total. Yohanna returns the pass with the receipt.

"Until next time, Dells."

Calla scoops up her flowers and seeds from the counter. We're almost out the door when I hear a quiet *psst*. Yohanna motions for me to come back. She reaches under the counter and hands me a packet of seeds. Petunias. I shake it, and the seeds scatter around inside.

"For the Lion," she whispers.

"Thanks, Yohanna." I look at the team pictures again. Underneath them is a short stack of shelves with rolls of receipt paper, cups of pens, and an old-looking cash register. There's a sticker on the side of the register, with letters so worn, I can barely read them: *Lakefest 2014.*

"Need something else?" Yohanna asks.

"I was looking at the sticker." I point, and she follows my finger to the register.

"Lakefest. Fun times. I had my first kiss at Lakefest. Meanwhile, you were running around in your unicorn bathing suit."

"Really?" I gasp.

Yohanna laughs. "Which part? The kiss or the magic horse?"

I feel the blush attack my skin. "The . . . kiss."

"Mm-hmm. Jacob Rosenbloom. Down by the water. Very dreamy."

Before I can stop it, I'm picturing Derek's face close to mine, our toes at the edge of the water. I shove the thought away so my imagination can't add more details. Yohanna's memory is just another reason to bring Lakefest back. Good things happened there.

"Say hypothetically I was trying to have another picnic. Would Poppyseed be interested in selling flowers and vegetables and things?" I make my voice as clear and professional as possible. It feels like I'm using a foreign accent.

"Hypothetically, I'd be there in a heartbeat," Yohanna answers.

My chest swells with the feeling of having done something right.

"And if it wasn't hypothetical?" I ask.

"Whatever you want us to do, we'll be there. You just let me know." She winks.

"Thank you so much, Yohanna. Thank you."

Yohanna smiles and sticks her tongue between the gap in her teeth.

"Little tip: When you go around and ask other people to help? Don't call it hypothetical if it's real. Have faith."

She's right. I have to stop thinking of my plan as a dream. I have to believe with everything inside me that it's going to happen.

I thank Yohanna again and burst out of Poppyseed like a sprouting flower. Calla is standing next to her car, scanning the parking lot. She spots me sprinting across the pavement.

"Where were you?" she asks when I make it to her. The violets sit in the back seat like passengers.

"Free seeds," I say, out of breath, and hand them over.

"Oh. Cool." She drops the seeds into her purse.

I don't tell Calla about Poppyseed being part of Lake-fest. Right now it really, truly feels like I can make this work. And I don't want her to tell me that I'm wrong.

My heart doesn't slow down the whole drive home.

CHAPTER SEVENTEEN

SKYLIGHT HOUSE

We plan to meet at Skylight House on Tuesday. Well, Marley doesn't call it Skylight House, obviously. She calls it the Rent It, which makes it feel like a cold, empty place and not the best of all the lake houses, where you can lie on the living room carpet and see the stars.

Derek bails at the last minute.

Need to help Abuela find her glasses. Fill me in later, B.

The excuse stings me through the phone. Abuela does constantly lose important belongings, but Derek should still be able to make our meeting. If Marley is bothered by the cancellation, or notices that Derek only addressed me, she doesn't show it.

No prob. Brooke, bring your science stuff. Might as well work on our project too.

Which is why I have my backpack at my feet when Dad parks in Flamingo House's driveway.

"She's staying in Skylight House," I remind him, pointing next door.

"I know. I'm meeting someone here. Can you walk over?"

My suspicion antennas go up. "Sure. Who are you meeting?"

Dad slides his hands over Gus's worn steering wheel.

"A Realtor. But don't get worked up. It's just a visit."

My insides go numb. Maybe it's just a visit now, but then what?

"Why would I get worked up?" I mumble.

I get out of the truck fast and run next door before Dad can say anything else. Thirteen days. That's all I have to stop the FOR SALE signs from popping up in the yards. I see the lake, wide and sparkling behind the houses, and run faster, straight through the front door of Skylight House.

A loud shriek greets me. Skylight House opens up to a long hall, and Marley is standing at the other end looking horrified. She drops a vanilla yogurt cup.

"You just scared the living crap out of me." She puts one

hand on her heart. The other holds a yogurt-coated spoon.

I rush down the hall, grabbing a tissue from the little shelf nearby.

"I'm so sorry. I'm not used to knocking here."

Marley stands frozen while I clean up the creamy spill with the tissue. All of a sudden, she starts laughing. She has a goose-honk laugh, and it's contagious. I can't help but giggle too. It's a funny, inside joke kind of moment, which I never expected to have with Marley.

"My house is your house," she says. She wipes the corner of her eye. "Literally."

"I owe you a yogurt," I answer, dropping the tissue into the garbage can.

We move to the living room, sink into the squishy beige couch. The skylight dumps warm sun onto our heads. Marley's books are spread out on the coffee table.

"This is Organizer Olivia's time line technique." She waves a hand over her setup. I can tell that we're straight back to business, but I have the sore abs to prove how hard we cracked up.

"What's the time line technique?" I ask. I feel guilty that Marley's blog posts are still unread in my locker. *Tomorrow I'll bring them home*, I tell myself. I'll put the reminder on my to-do list and then check that little box. Not that I've used the to-do list Marley helped me make either . . .

"You set your to-dos in the order you need to finish them. I put the new paragraphs for our poster over here, because we need to cut those out first, and then my textbook is here so I can pull out some more facts, and then Lakefest ideas over here." She has three lists with different labels on top—*entertainment, food, advertising.*

Nerves churn in my stomach. I've been so happy about getting the yes from Poppyseed that I forgot there's still tons to do. Like, you know, *telling people about Lakefest*!

"Good idea," I say. "Speaking of the picnic, the flower shop is interested in . . ."

I trail off, because Marley has a finger over her lips.

"Cockroaches first."

A little voice in my head whispers, *Okay, Bossy Floss.* I tell it to shut up. She's not bossy—at least, not totally. I think she just wants us to succeed. I open my binder, and a loose paper slips out. It lands faceup near Marley's leg. The crumpled, checkless to-do list. Marley glances at the list, then back at her time line technique on the table.

I think a dark thought. It comes out once in a while, when I've done something extra disappointing. *I am the worst.* Marley has been trying to help me this whole time—with the blogs, with the list. And I haven't used any of her tips.

"Sorry about that." I push the paper back into my

binder and try to explain. "It really was helpful. I just forgot to cross things off."

I wait for her temper to flare like in that gym class volleyball game. Three, two, one . . .

Marley shrugs. "Different techniques work for different people."

If I can't even keep track of things in the simplest way, then there must be no hope for me.

Marley takes out her phone. When she leans it against a pencil cup a minute later, a girl with tan skin and waist-length black hair is paused on the screen. Marley presses play.

"Hey there, Olivia-nizers! I'm back with another video, and I think it's a pretty fun one. We're going to take a test!"

I look at our table full of work. Why would Marley pull up this video now? And who would think a test was fun?

"I thought we were working on our project," I say.

Marley hands me a paper with four typed paragraphs, and a pair of scissors.

"We're multitasking."

I take the materials from her and tune back in to the video. Maybe Marley isn't mad. She's not trying to cut me with the scissors or anything, which seems like a good sign.

"It's not like a school test, I swear." Organizer Olivia shakes her long hair. *"It's a test to see what your organization*

style is. I'll ask you five questions and give you three possible answers. Your job is to answer honestly, and to keep track of whether you choose mostly A, B, or C."

The letters pop up in shimmery pink text next to Olivia's head, and she points to them one by one.

"Are you going to take the test too?" I ask Marley.

"I've done it already." She uncaps a highlighter and settles back in the sofa with her notebook. "I'm mostly A's."

I listen to Olivia's questions while I cut the paragraphs out.

"Here we go with question one. How would people describe you? A, efficient; B, scattered; C, helpful."

I mark a little *B* in my notebook. Marley said she's mostly A's, which means she probably chose "efficient." By the last question, I've answered three B's and one C.

"Last one," Olivia announces. The video lets out a fog-horn sound. *"What is your biggest fear? A, losing control; B, disappointing others; or C, being still."*

I don't know what the question has to do with organization, but I do know my answer: B. I make the final mark in my notebook.

"What were you?" Marley asks. She copies down words from the textbook.

"Mostly B's." I form my four cutout paragraphs into a pile.

"I thought so."

Her answer burns in my belly. She thinks she knows

me, but she doesn't. It reminds me of Calla, thinking she knows what's best, not realizing how much I need her to be my big sister instead of a replacement mom. How much I need her to stop talking about junior year and college because I just want her here right now.

"Listen to the explanations," Marley says. She says it shyly. Like she's not trying to push too hard but doesn't want me to turn off the video.

I tune back in.

"All my A's out there, you're the direct *style of organization. You are all about lists, and checking items off that list. Some people might call you intense. You may call yourself a perfectionist. But you just know how to get things done! Find a way to communicate your ideas, but remember that other people have ideas too! You are a reliable, responsible star. Good for you!"*

The Lakefest lists Marley put together sit in front of me. Marley *can* be a little intense, but she's going to help me pull off this picnic. Which basically makes her a superhero.

"My B's, you are the creatives! *You are visual, and have HUGE goals. Unfortunately, that means the smaller tasks don't appeal to you as much, so sometimes you might not do them. Maybe some people call you a procrastinator? Find an*

aesthetically appealing way to keep track of what you want to do. Bullet journals are a great choice for the creative type, and so is writing down your big goals, as a reminder of what you're reaching for."

Creative? I can't draw or play music or write beautiful poems. I think Organizer Olivia needs to adjust her quiz. Plus, I don't really appreciate being called a procrastinator.

Even if I am.

"What do you think?" Marley asks.

"It's interesting. I don't think I'd call myself a creative type, but she seems cool to watch."

Organizer Olivia clears her throat like I interrupted her.

"C's, are you still there? I'm not sure, because you're the active *type. You jump into things right away. There's no need for lists for you, because once a task enters your head, you have to do it. Try to sloooooooow down. The world needs your energy, but you have to rest once in a while."*

Calla's face pops into my head. Organizer Olivia is describing *her.* She doesn't stop moving: going to her clubs, taking care of her garden, doing chores for me and Dad. Calla jumped into filling Mom's role right after she died and hasn't slowed down since.

"I think it's the big-goal part of being a creative type that fits you," Marley says.

I laugh. Not the way Marley and I did when I first got here, but enough to make her look at me with her forehead wrinkled.

"It's just, I can barely get my dirty clothes into the laundry basket," I explain. Organizer Olivia says goodbye to her viewers, and the video goes dark.

"But you want to plan a huge picnic for the town in thirteen days."

She says it matter-of-factly. Her words click into place one by one, like the combination to a lock.

"That is technically true."

Marley stacks our project notes on the table.

"Don't underestimate yourself," she says. It feels warmer than her usual instructions. It's the good kind of command, like Coach Tanaka gives.

I'm about to thank her, maybe tell her that she really is a "reliable, responsible star," like Olivia said, when the front door creaks open. The click of high heels echoes in the hall, until a blond woman in a pink pencil skirt appears.

"Your father has outdone himself. Absolutely outdone himself!" She drops into a kitchen chair.

"Mom, we have company," Marley mumbles. She points at me.

"I see that, Marley. I have eyes." She kicks her heels off

under the table. "But this whole town is already chattering about it, so I might as well spread the news myself."

The rumor about Marley's mom swoops through my brain. To be honest, she seems capable of taking a chain saw to a tooth-shaped shrub.

"Can you not?" Marley begs her mom.

Skylight House has never felt so uncomfortable. I want to run out of the room as fast as I ran in.

"I'm Brooke," I say instead of escaping.

Marley's mom starts rubbing her feet. "Hi, Brooke. I'm Dr. Macintosh. When was your last dental cleaning?"

"Uh . . ."

"Mom!"

Marley throws me a mortified look. Things were awkward with her dad the other night at Papa Margherita's, but this doesn't seem much better.

"Fine. I can tell when I'm not wanted." Dr. Macintosh sulks as she walks to the bedroom off the kitchen.

The house goes quiet. Marley stares at the time line of tasks on the table like it doesn't make sense anymore. I get a weird urge to tell her about what happened at the concession stand with the slushie boys who rated me a two, just to let her know that I've felt small and embarrassed too.

I decide to change the subject instead.

"Should we talk about Lakefest?" I ask.

Marley straightens her shoulders. The skylight above us shows nothing but blue.

"Of course."

Late that night, I'm awake, and Calla is a mound of flannel comforter beneath the string lights over her bed. She won't admit that they're night-lights but it's the truth. Calla is afraid of the dark. I take out my earbuds as quietly as I can, and start to watch Organizer Olivia's video again.

I re-answer the questions. My result is the same: creative style. I still flinch at the procrastination part, but I manage to focus on the good stuff. I don't have a notebook nearby, so I use the Notes app on my phone to write down my big goals, like Olivia said to.

Big goals: Stop Dad from selling the lake houses. Remind Calla of a time before she went into Mom mode. Make Lakefest happen so my family will remember what it was like when we were happy.

I can't help but wonder if my goals are too big. Maybe even impossible.

CHAPTER EIGHTEEN
DEALS AT THE DELI COUNTER

Derek and I have practice at the same time on Wednesday, so I go home with him and his mom, Doris. She tells us she needs cilantro, and we stop at La Manzana on the way. It's the only Hispanic food market in Lincoln. It's smaller than the chain stores, and cozier inside. The air is warm and smells like garlic and onions instead of sterile cleaning products. Display cases line the whole right side of the store. I spot the rice and stewed meats La Manzana makes every morning.

My legs are still sore from practice. I shake them out.

"Catcher legs?" Derek asks. Sweat mats his curls to his forehead.

"Yeah, I'm going to have arthritis before the age of thirteen."

"Want me to carry you?" He laughs, but in a maybe-not-actually-joking way.

It takes all my brain power to keep from saying yes.

Doris saves me by shoving a shopping basket between us. Derek grabs it.

"We could use some cold cuts. Go to the deli and ask for a half pound each of turkey and ham." She reaches into her alligator-print purse and pulls out a stack of coupons. She hands one to me. It's for some kind of green tea sparkling water. "And see if you can find that."

Doris likes to try new stuff when it's on sale, and makes Derek and me find which aisle it's in, like we're on a treasure hunt for discounted items. She takes her shopping basket and heads for the produce section. Derek and I walk to the deli counter. It's in the back corner, at the end of the rows of prepared foods. We're almost there when a set of double doors opens behind the counter and an employee steps out.

"It's Robby," I whisper, my heart rate spiking at the sight of him. I haven't seen him since that day on our front steps.

Derek whips his head around. As if Robby might be on the ceiling.

"Behind the counter, D."

Robby starts wiping the meat slicer with a towel. He's

wearing a hairnet under his baseball hat, and plastic gloves on his hands.

Derek slowly turns his hat around to match Robby's, but I pretend not to notice.

"Hey," I say to Robby when we get to the counter. It feels too casual for someone whose sister broke his heart, but I don't know if there's any good greeting for this situation.

Robby's shoulders jump up. He spins around. His startled expression fades when he recognizes me.

"Brooke, you can't be sneaking up on people near a slicer. That's how Butcher Benito lost his thumb!" He inspects his gloved hands like he's making sure all his fingers are still accounted for.

"That would be awful. I know you need those hands in left field," Derek says. Or gushes, really. Robby chuckles.

"Yeah, I like 'em." His cool rays are as potent as the smell of La Manzana's rice and beans.

"When did you start working here?" I ask.

"Last week." Robby clears his throat. "Needed something to keep me busy. And extra money doesn't hurt."

"Awesome," Derek cuts in. "Can you hook us up with half a pound each of ham and turkey?"

Robby smiles while I cringe. I think Derek feels around

Robby the same thing I feel around Lily: a desperate need to be liked. But Robby is the opposite of Lily. He uses his cool rays for good, not evil.

"I should be able to handle that."

Robby pulls a plastic-wrapped ham from the chilled case in front of him and brings it back to the machine. His arm moves up and down, up and down, and every slice fills me with more sympathy. I shouldn't have eavesdropped on his conversation with Calla. It's hard to watch people do everyday things when you know how much they're hurting. Like Dad taking out the trash or checking the mail right after Mom died. I could practically see the weight sitting on his shoulders.

Robby drops the sliced ham onto the scale in front of us. It's half a pound exactly. He puts the meat into a bag and slaps a sticker onto the outside, then moves on to the turkey.

While Robby slices and Derek shifts his position a thousand times, I study the food that fills the display case. There are loaves of fresh bread, potatoes in deep red sauce, fried pork chops with the bones sticking out. They're all lined up like one big buffet at a picnic table.

An idea flashes into my mind.

"D, let's have La Manzana do the food for Lakefest," I say.

Derek quits his posing and looks at me. "I thought we were having Papa Margherita's."

"Marley did say that we could do something new. Highlight a different business. We can help spread the word about this place."

"And whatever Marley says, we have to do, right?"

I scrunch my face at him. "That's not what I meant."

Robby comes back with the pile of turkey. Derek shoves his hands deep into his pockets and stares at the floor. I don't think he's trying to look cool anymore.

"Can I speak to your manager?" I ask Robby.

He pauses in the middle of zipping the bag of turkey.

"Not a fan of my customer service?" He raises one eyebrow. I can picture Derek trying that move in the mirror.

"I want to talk to them about . . . a business opportunity."

Robby's expression switches from confused to impressed. "Benito went home for the night. He showed me how to close the store. What if you give me your pitch and I pass it on to him?"

I try to remember the speaking points Marley went over with me yesterday—the picnic is good for the community, and being part of it would be beneficial for the business.

"It's Lakefest. We're bringing it back. Would La Manzana be interested in doing the food? It's on May fifteenth, which I know is short notice, but we think it will be worth it."

Robby nods, rubs his chin.

"Is Calla going to be there? Helping you and stuff?" he asks.

I didn't expect that. I was prepared for questions about how much food we'd need (based on the picnics in the past, enough for at least a hundred people) or how La Manzana would make money from it (Marley said we should charge ten dollars per adult and five dollars for kids). But I still haven't told Calla about any of the Lakefest plans, so I have no clue if she'll be there. Or if she'll help me.

But Robby doesn't need to know that. If he thinks Calla will be there, maybe he'll try harder to get La Manzana on board. And maybe, if I can get Calla there, there's another miracle that Lakefest can grant: getting Robby and Calla back together.

"Yeah, of course. She's all about it," I tell him.

Robby smiles, and I instantly regret my fib. I feel Derek's squinted eyes on the side of my face.

"I'll talk to Benito tomorrow. I know he'll be into it. And I can DJ for you. I have my own setup." He takes a black marker and writes his phone number on the bag of turkey before handing it to Derek. "Keep me posted."

"Thanks, Robby," I say, my throat tight around the words.

"Anytime."

"I'll text you," Derek says, finding his voice again. He points to the number on the turkey bag.

Robby waves and disappears through the doors to the kitchen. I want to feel another swell of pride, like I did at Poppyseed, but a guilt snake coils around my neck instead. Robby's being so nice to me, the way he's always been, and I lied to him about Calla anyway. But time is running out, and with his help we can cross food and entertainment off our Lakefest list.

"Didn't Calla think Lakefest was a bad idea?" Derek asks.

"It's going to be fine. I know she'll show up." I don't know who I'm trying to convince, myself or Derek.

Derek doesn't push the subject. "Time to hunt for bargains."

I take Doris's coupon out of my pocket. "Let's do it."

We search through the aisles. At La Manzana, the groceries aren't always where you expect them to be. While we look, Derek tells me about a hard test he had in math class, and how Abuela's dentures are missing again. The talk of fake teeth reminds me of Marley.

I want to ask Derek what he has against her. I want to ask about the day we folded sheets in Flamingo House. I want to ask if he gets butterflies around me, and if it scares him half to death. But I focus my attention on our hunt for green tea sparkling water, until we find it mixed in with the canned soups.

CHAPTER NINETEEN
BACK AND FORTH

Dad gets home at around five on Thursday night. He asks me if I want to practice throws in the backyard, and I'm running to my bat bag in the garage before he can finish his sentence. We haven't played catch since the season started. He usually works until after dark, at the houses or the accounting office or both.

We get set about thirty feet apart in the grass. Second-base throws are longer than that, but when we're in the backyard instead of on a field, we stand closer together so we can talk. Sometimes I think about how many balls went over Dad's head when I was learning to throw. He'd have to chase them down. It must have been annoying, but he never made it seem that way.

"Ready?" I ask.

Dad gives me a thumbs-up with his free hand and

shakes his glove with the other. His glove is so old, I'm surprised it doesn't fall apart. I grip the green softball and toss my first throw. Dad snags it easily.

"Remind me, when does the championship tournament start?" Dad asks. He throws the ball back to me and I catch it. Dad's throws are always direct and firm.

"May twelfth. We play the J and B Funeral Home Bashers." My next throw is a little wobbly. I hate playing the Bashers. We had Mom's wake at J&B, and when I see their jersey, it puts thoughts into my head that I don't want. I hope my saying the name now doesn't do the same to Dad.

"Can't wait to watch you win that third title in a row." Dad throws the ball high this time—a practice pop fly. I find it in the air and position myself under it, not looking away until it's safe in my glove. "Nice one."

"Thanks," I say. "To both things."

We throw the ball back and forth. The only sounds are the crickets and the ball smacking our gloves. I'm never this quiet around Dad. Lately all the things I want to talk to him about feel too big: Lakefest, Realtors, Calla. But now that the picnic is starting to come together, I can't hide it anymore. I need Dad's approval. And help. Without him, there is no lawn, no lake. It will just be *Fest*.

"Dad, remember when you said if I told you the truth, you wouldn't be mad at me?"

He squints and takes a step toward me.

"What happened, Brooke?"

The softball is squeezed tight inside my glove, like a stress ball. I take a breath.

"I've started working on Lakefest. I have Poppyseed involved, and an idea for food, and music. My friend Marley is helping a lot, and Derek, and I really think we can pull it off and I just need you to say yes to letting us use the lawns for the day."

I throw the ball back to him, putting the ball into his court. Or glove, technically. He catches it without taking his eyes off me.

"You could have told me sooner," he says.

"I knew you didn't think I could do it."

Dad pauses mid-throw.

"I believe you can do anything, Brookie. I just didn't want you to get too overwhelmed or disappointed. It's a big undertaking. A lot can go wrong."

"I can handle it," I tell him.

He waits a second longer. Behind him, the sky is hazy blue. "When will it be?"

"May fifteenth."

Dad's expression seems to change ten times in one second. He goes from shocked to serious to smiling.

"If there's any day that will bring you good luck," he says, "it's that one. I'll let the renters know there's an event on the properties that day."

I go over to his side of the lawn, hold out my glove, tap it against his. The softball version of a hug. When I was younger, I would try on Dad's glove for fun. It was so big on me that I was convinced Dad was superhuman.

I still think he is.

CHAPTER TWENTY

THE SCOUT MOTTO

I wait outside the cafeteria for Derek and Marley. She texted us last night to say she had news. Class just got out, so I'm swarmed by other seventh graders going to lunch. The smell of fried food is thick in the air. I spot Marley in the crowd. She joins me by the wall with papers in her hands.

"Here." Marley gives half to me. The stack is still printer warm. I read the top sheet, immediately struck by the big blue bubble letters. *You're Invited to Lakefest!* Smaller fireworks shapes have details inside—the date, the entrance fees, the fact that Robby will be the DJ. A sentence on the bottom says to contact me or Marley with any questions.

"Wow, it's awesome!" My voice is a borderline squeal.

Marley swipes her bangs to the side, smiles.

"We'll put them on all the bulletin boards. I got permission from the office already."

I see Derek in a group of other players from the junior leagues. Lily is there, talking to the baseball player beside him. She giggles loud enough to fill the hall. I wave to Derek. He waves back, but barely, and his eyes shift between me and his group. Like he's not sure if he knows me. They get closer until I can reach out and tap his arm.

"D," I say.

He sneaks out of the group to stand with us. "Hey, I'm going to lunch."

Suspicion crawls up my spine. Derek definitely answered Marley's text with a thumbs-up emoji.

"We're putting up Lakefest flyers," I tell him.

Marley tries to give some of her papers to him. He reads the top one, then looks toward the cafeteria. Lily and the rest of them have disappeared down the stairs.

"My name's not on it," he says.

I rush to read the bottom sentence again. *Text Brooke D or Marley M for more information.* No mention of Derek.

"Derek, I'm sorry, I—" Marley starts to apologize.

"It's cool, I'm starving. You can do it without me. I'll help with the next thing."

Marley shuffles the papers back into her pile, and I try to understand this cold Derek in front of me. It's a stone-statue version of him, a version who doesn't laugh, or call me B, or maybe-almost-kiss me in a room with flamingo wallpaper.

"Okay, you'd better," I say.

He nods and dashes to the cafeteria, leaving me in a cloud of questions.

"He really doesn't like me," Marley says.

My heart thumps. I should have known that she would pick up on Derek's weird vibes.

"No," I say quickly. "Wait, I mean, he doesn't *not* like you."

Marley clears her throat. "You don't have to say that. Likeable people don't usually get nicknames like Bossy Floss."

It's painful enough to keep the mean things people say inside your head, so Marley saying the words out loud must hurt even more. After those slushie boys teased me, I stared at the mirror and thought *two out of ten, two out of ten* until my eyes were so blurred with tears, I couldn't see myself anymore.

"I like you, Marley," I say.

Marley smiles at the bulletin board hung next to the cafeteria doors, then pulls a clear box of thumbtacks out of her back pocket. She pins the Lakefest flyer in a blank spot near the center. It stands out from the other papers like a slice of blue sky among gray clouds.

"I'll take your word for it."

Lincoln Middle School is shaped like a big square with

one walkway that cuts through the center. The next bulletin board is by the main office. Everyone's made it to lunch or their next class by now, so it's just us in the hall.

"The same ad is going to run in the newspaper," Marley tells me while we walk. "My parents do that for their office."

"Marley! Isn't that expensive?"

Marley shrugs. "My dad helped."

My mind replays Marley's dad paying for Derek's and my pizza. I guess he isn't done sucking up to her yet. I wonder what it is he needs forgiveness for, but don't ask.

"That was nice of him," I say.

"Sure."

We turn the corner where the main office is. This bulletin board is fuller than the first one. The only open space is on the bottom. Marley hands me a piece of tape, and I stick the flyer to the spongy cork. It hangs off the edge.

"It's not at eyeline, but it will do," Marley says.

"How do you know all this stuff? I've never thought about anything being at eyeline."

"Of course you have. You play softball. You'd end up with a black eye if you didn't." She pauses mid-step. "But I learned a lot about event planning in Girl Scouts."

We're in the eighth-grade hall now. I hear snippets of lessons from the classrooms.

"My sister, Calla, did Girl Scouts. Now she does just about every club on the planet," I say.

"It's good to feel like you're part of something."

I *hmmph* so loudly that Marley turns her head. Her eyes look for an explanation.

"I don't think that's why she does it. She says it's because it's junior year, but sometimes I think she's just staying busy to avoid her feelings."

Marley has tape too, so she sticks a flyer to a wall where there's no bulletin board.

"Active type, huh?"

I think about how people become friends. With Derek, it was because his abuela babysat us and we grew up side by side. With Kasey and Aimi, we all love softball. How did it happen for Marley and me? Is it these little moments of understanding exactly what each other is talking about?

"The *most* active of them all."

We put flyers on the boards by the gym and the art room and the library. I copy Marley's move and start posting them on the walls, too. By the time we get close to the cafeteria again, we've pasted the whole school with the news that Lakefest is back.

"There's still time for Nugget Friday," I say. I can see the bulletin board where we started up ahead.

"It's more of a ham-and-cheese-sandwich Friday for me."

"I'll share."

She stops short in front of the bulletin board. Her eyebrows pull together.

"Really? You don't have to."

Sharing lunch means we'll have to sit together. I try to picture Marley at the sports table, talking to everyone, dunking nuggets into ketchup. But my brain screams, *EVERYONE WILL STARE AT YOU.*

"You didn't have to help me with Lakefest. It's sort of the least I can do," I say.

She smiles, but not for long. Her eyes laser-focus on the center of the bulletin board. I'm afraid to see what she's looking at. I turn my head a little so I can barely see it, like when I watch horror movies through my fingers.

Someone drew in the space between the top part of the *f* so that it looks like *LakePest.* Marley's name is crossed out, the letters *B.F.* scrawled in its place.

Bossy Floss.

The flyer twists my heart into a knot. I consider sprinting around the school, tearing down all the flyers, forgetting about planning this event with Marley. But maybe *this* is how I become friends with Marley. By treating her like one.

Plus, running isn't allowed in the halls.

"When Calla was a Girl Scout, she told me the scout motto," I say.

Marley finally looks away from those painful initials. "Be prepared?"

I nod. "Be prepared."

I take my last thumbtack and hang a new flyer right over the ruined one.

CHAPTER TWENTY-ONE
EXTRA WHIPPED CREAM

Every year, Lincoln High holds an ice cream social to raise money for prom. Calla is working the event this year as part of the student council. Dad gets out of the office late on Monday, so we show up an hour after the starting time. The line for ice cream wraps around the cafeteria. I spot Calla at the end of the serving station, squirting whipped cream on top of sundaes.

"We better get in line if we want ice cream in this century," Dad says.

"Yeah, in the next century ice cream might be made of space plasma."

Dad laughs. We go back and forth while we wait in line, coming up with theories of what a sundae would be like in the year 3000. I ignore the purple bags under Dad's eyes and let myself sink into our jokes. We're almost to the front when someone calls Dad's name from the tables. Papa Margherita is waving him down. His daughter is in Calla's grade.

"I'm going to see what Jensen needs," Dad says as he steps out of line. "Can you grab me a sundae and I'll meet you at a table?"

I accept the task and watch him walk away until the large man behind me clears his throat.

The serving table is set up in stations—bowls and spoons, then ice creams, then toppings. I pick cookie dough for me and chocolate for Dad. The server digs out the frozen scoops, his face beet-red. He's out of breath when he drops the ice cream into my bowl.

"We could have thawed these a little," he mumbles to the girl next to him.

Calla smiles when I get to her station.

"Whipped cream me, please," I say.

"It's my honor." She tilts the can and squeezes the tip over both bowls. The creamy deliciousness splooshes onto the ice cream. "Where's Dad?"

"Talking to Jensen."

The pink-haired girl next to Calla shakes her whipped cream can.

"We're going to need more soon," she says.

Calla slams her own can onto the table. "Got it!" She pulls her plastic gloves off.

The girl blinks. "You don't have to do it right now. I just meant—"

"Don't worry, I'll be back." Calla rushes toward the kitchen doors on the other side of the cafeteria. The girl stares at me, her eyeshadow black and blue. I want to tell her that Calla's an active type, that she can't stop moving, but I'm not sure this girl would understand.

The large man clears his throat again, and I scurry away. The cafeteria suddenly feels huge. I get first-day-of-school nerves, when you don't know where your friends are sitting during lunch yet. Dad is still talking to Jensen at a full table. The sundaes numb my hands.

"You okay, Brooke?" A voice soars in to rescue me.

I turn and see Robby with an empty bowl. He's wearing the orange Orioles jersey that Dad got him. His sneakers have matching orange laces.

"Oh, yeah, I was just trying to find someone I know."

Robby spreads his arms out. "You found him."

He motions for me to follow him to the garbage cans in the corner. Robby walks so tall, it makes me unslouch my own shoulders.

"I've been meaning to text you. Benito's got his menu planned for Lakefest. He'll do ten trays of rice and beans, three meats, and salad, for ten percent of your profits. Sound all right?"

"It's more than all right. It's incredible. Thank you so much, Robby."

He smiles and turns to dump his bowl into the trash. Over his shoulder I see Calla emerging from the kitchen with four cans of whipped cream clutched to her chest.

"You want to sit with me?" he asks.

Robby's facing the wrong way to see Calla, for Calla to see him. But this is my chance. If Lakefest is going to bring them back together, I have to start now.

I walk directly at Robby, pushing him toward Calla. His eyes go round and he backs up. As if I could really run him over.

"You're acting a little funny, Brooke," he says, still back-pedaling.

"What?" I say, acting oblivious, still charging forward. "Am I?"

I've pushed him far enough. Robby turns around, winds up face-to-face with Calla. Calla looks like she's locked eyes with a ghost. A whipped cream can slips from her grasp to the floor, and Robby reaches down fast like he's snagging a ground ball. He hands it to her.

"Thanks," Calla says. She stares at Robby for one more

second, then speeds to the table to finish her delivery.

Well, that didn't work. Robby runs a hand over his head, his jaw squeezed tight.

I see Larissa walking away from the ice cream line with her mom, the high school guidance counselor.

"My friend just got here. I'll talk to you soon." I leave Robby alone with whatever thoughts are running through his head. Even after I catch up with Larissa and we settle at a table, he's still standing in the same spot.

Larissa's mom asks us about school and softball, but she does it in a way that doesn't feel like we're being interrogated. The cafeteria clears out slowly. Larissa and her mom leave after a while. Dad is still with Jensen, and his sundae sits beside me, a chocolate puddle. Robby is back at a table. He's the only one not laughing hysterically at whatever his friend just said.

The sound of a whipped cream squirt snaps me out of my loneliness. Calla leaves a dollop in my bowl, then takes the empty spot next to me, in front of Dad's melted ice cream.

"It looked like you could use some," she says.

I dip my pinky into the white swirl and lick it off.

"Always," I say.

She twists the whipped cream cap in her hands. Her pink nail polish is chipped.

"Hey, what were you talking to Robby about?"

My ears prick up. Did my not-so-graceful plan work after all?

"Lakefest. I know I haven't told you yet, but I'm going through with it. Dad said yes."

Calla's eyebrows pull together. "He really doesn't have time for that, Brooke."

"I have it all taken care of. I've organized almost everything."

"You? You, who would lose your head if it wasn't attached?"

I let Calla's comment slide over me. I'm in the middle of a mission, and I don't have time for hurt feelings.

"Yup, me. Robby has been a huge help, though. Huge! He got the food set up for us, and he's going to DJ."

Calla looks a little impressed. She fixes her eyes on his table.

"That's really nice of him."

As if he can sense her staring, Robby looks up and smiles the widest smile I've ever seen. He lifts his fingers in a wave. Like a miracle, Calla waves back.

"You'll come to Lakefest, right? It wouldn't feel right without you there."

I hold my breath and wait. All the worst answers march

through my head: *I have a cooking club meeting. I have SAT prep. I don't care about the lake anymore.*

"I'll be there." She stands, and my heart starts waving a victory flag. "Tell Dad I said bye and I'll be home by nine. And if your laundry is on the floor when I get there, I may actually lose my mind."

I focus on the *I'll be there* instead of her mom voice. She gives me one more dollop of whipped cream before snapping the top on and leaving, and it's as sweet as my plan falling into place. Not too long after, Dad finds me and says we can go. We drive down the dark streets toward home.

"Sorry for ditching you in there, Brookie. But I think you'll be happy to hear that Jensen can donate pizzas to the picnic." Dad lets out a little whoop.

"We got La Manzana to do the food," I tell him.

"Have you forgotten the number one rule of Lakefest?"

I crinkle my forehead. " 'Wear sunscreen'?"

Dad laughs, and the windows are down, and the world feels right for a second.

"That's a good one. But no. It's 'the more the merrier.' "

I can't believe how everything is coming together. Calla is at least on waving terms with Robby. We're going to have enough food. Dad seems totally on board.

But what if it all falls apart?

Things can be going great until they aren't anymore. I think that was the hardest part of losing Mom. We were right in the middle of our story, right in the middle of being a happy family, and then it just ended.

CHAPTER TWENTY-TWO

REASONS TO RUN

Derek and I go into his backyard to play catch on Tuesday but end up lying in the grass, looking for shapes in the clouds. Our gloves wait patiently by our sides.

"Rhino," Derek says. He points to a big cloud with a hornlike curve sticking out.

"That's a stretch," I say.

"Hey." Derek nudges me with his elbow. "Anything goes in cloud watching."

"You're right. Reindeer." I point to a cloud that has no shape at all.

Derek nods. "I can see that."

I laugh out loud. Derek moves his hand from his chest to the grass. It lands an inch away from mine. The sun on my face is suddenly too hot, so I shoot upright.

"Lakefest is going to be great, D," I say. I need to distract myself from the heat.

Derek stays put on the ground, his eyes still on the clouds.

"I'm sure." His voice is flat. I glance at him.

"You don't sound sure."

He shifts his body to face me. The grass rustles against his gray T-shirt.

"I just don't know much about it."

My eyebrows arch to the sky. "What? You're part of it!"

"The flyer doesn't say so." He plucks a piece of grass and tosses it in my direction.

"I'm sorry, D. Marley probably didn't think it would be a big deal."

Derek rolls his eyes.

"It's really not a big deal. But . . ." He grits his teeth like he's trying to stop words from escaping. "I don't want people to start making fun of you, too."

His statement hits me like a fastball to the face. So it isn't really about the flyers. I know Derek wants to be cool like Robby, but I didn't realize how important it is to him. Important enough to distance himself from Lakefest.

"Marley's been helping me a lot," I say.

"I get it. She's helping with the picnic. When that's over, will things go back to normal?"

I shake my head.

"It's more than that. She's helped me, like, understand myself more." I take a breath. "I'm a creative type. I procrastinate a lot, but I care about the big picture. I'm a dreamer."

The word "dreamer" feels silly in my mouth. Derek sits up, still facing me. He doesn't look like he thinks it's funny.

"What does that mean?"

"I always want to do more, be better. And I'm hard on myself when I'm not. Like when I forget homework or put off my chores and stuff."

Derek shakes his bent legs up and down.

"I didn't know that," he says.

"I didn't really know it either."

Only a sliver of sunlight separates Derek and me. His legs keep fluttering, and so do the butterfly wings in my stomach.

"Is there anything else I don't know about you?" He scoots in until the sun sliver disappears.

Our faces are as close as they were in Flamingo House.

"No. Is there anything I don't know about you?"

"Yeah."

Derek leans in. Slowly. His pink lips start to pucker. It's happening. I'm going to have my first kiss ever. I'm going to kiss my best friend in the whole world. I inch toward him too, closer and closer, until I can see the pores of his cheeks.

And then I twist away, end up sprawled in the grass.

It's Derek. This can't happen with Derek.

My glove presses into my hip. I'm all mixed up, like I've been through a slushie machine. I stumble to my feet and start to run.

"Wait! B!" Derek calls.

He's fast, faster than me, and soon he's close behind. I crush dandelions under my feet.

Derek stops chasing me at the end of his driveway.

"I'm sorry!" he shouts to me. "Please come back!"

"I have to go, Derek."

I keep running down the street, toward home. His full name feels strange in my mouth. My mouth feels strange now that it's been almost-kissed. Derek's duplex disappears behind me. I run faster than I ever have. I think I might beat the Olympic record for the mile between his house and mine.

A fire truck comes rushing past on my left. I press myself closer to the trees that line the road. The sirens blare like the truck is on its way to a disaster. I want to wave my arms to flag them down, let them know that they just left the biggest disaster behind.

CHAPTER TWENTY-THREE

BUNNY SLIPPERS AND COCKROACHES

Dad and I drive to the lake houses the next day. It's three o'clock, close to practice time, but Dad scheduled a quick meeting with the Realtor. I'm too confused about what happened with Derek yesterday to be bummed about the houses getting sold. Bodies can only hold so many emotions at once, right? It's science. I should ask Mrs. Valencia about it. I ignored Derek at school all day and sat with Marley during lunch at her spot near the vending machines.

"Good news! The renters that reserved the weekend of Lakefest are all okay with the event," Dad says, turning into the circle. "But I couldn't get ahold of the guest in number twenty-five. Madeline P."

Hearing Mom's first name adds *pain* to my feelings flurry. I'm going to overflow, like one of those baking soda volcanoes.

"What should we do?" I ask.

Dad parks on the curb in front of Fireplace House. A man waits on the front steps. His shiny black suit matches his car.

"Go talk to her in person."

We both get out of the car. Dad goes to meet the Realtor, and I walk to Skylight House. If I'm going to go talk to Madeline P, I'll need support.

I remember to knock this time.

Dr. Macintosh answers the door. She wears a white coat, a black skirt, and bunny slippers.

"You're the girl who owns the houses, right?" she asks.

Not for long, a dark voice in my mind answers.

"My family does."

"If I were to ask your dad which credit card is being charged for our rental, would he be able to tell me?"

A chill runs up my spine. I feel like I'm in the very wrong place at the very wrong time.

"Um. I have no idea. Is Marley here?"

Dr. Macintosh rubs her pointy chin.

"No." She opens the door wider. Her bunny slippers stare at me. "I only ask because my husband is known to be sneaky. Secret credit cards. The fling with our dental assistant. I'm sure you already know about that."

Marley isn't around to stop her mom from spilling all their secrets.

"I haven't heard anything." I start to back away from the door.

"Oh, really? No one has whispered to you about the 'Messy Macintoshes'?" She puts the last part in exaggerated air quotes.

Only that you went all Texas Chainsaw Massacre *on a tooth.*

"I have to go, Dr. Macintosh."

I walk fast toward the next lawn. I want to run, but it'll look like I'm fleeing the scene.

"I'm not as bad as they say!" she calls behind me.

I raise my arm so she'll know I heard her, but I don't stop until I'm on the front steps of Flamingo House. Out of the corner of my eye, I see Dr. Macintosh go back inside. I press the doorbell. It rings to the first three notes of "Hot Cross Buns."

No sound comes from inside, and there's no car in the driveway. I've just decided Madeline P isn't here and that I should give up and wait for Dad in the car, when the door opens.

A woman with snow-white hair appears. She's wearing a dress that looks like a quilt, and a tangle of gold necklaces.

"Are you selling cookies, dear?" she asks. She has a strong British accent.

"No, Ms. . . . . P," I answer, realizing I don't know her

last name. "My dad, Jonas Dell, is who you're renting this house from."

Her wrinkled hand wraps around the doorknob. "I think I followed all the check-in rules. That Rent-a-What website can be a little confusing."

I shake my head. "You didn't do anything wrong. On May fifteenth we're going to have a picnic. Out by the lake. Which means that there will be people on the lawn."

Madeline's silvery eyebrows inch together.

"I'm a writer, dear. Working on my next novel in the Goldie Locksmith mystery collection. Have you heard of it?"

I shake my head. Madeline smiles.

"I thought not. It's too noisy to write in the city. I came here for the peace and quiet."

Today is not my day. First Dad's meeting with the Realtor, then Marley not being home, and now I'm sure Madeline P is about to tell me that she doesn't want guests in the yard. Lakefest will have a huge gap in it.

"It will only be a few hours long, and not very loud." I sound like I'm begging, but I guess that's because I am. "Just a polite crowd, and some music. We won't bother you at all."

Madeline crosses her arms, still smiling, like it's a permanent part of her face.

"Did you hear me, dear? I'm a writer."

I don't want to be frustrated at this old woman who

shares Mom's name, but my hands curl into fists anyway. I hide them behind my back. "Yes. I heard you. I hope you enjoy your stay."

She leans closer to me, and her necklaces rattle. Behind her, Flamingo House is all cleaned up from the last time I saw it.

"Being a writer means never missing a chance to meet new characters," she says, and winks.

Hope blooms in my chest.

"Really?" I ask.

Madeline tosses her hands up. "Of course! Bring them on! Bring them in for tea. Whatever you want."

The hope is a full-blown flower now. I want to hug Madeline P; I want to cannonball into the lake. I stay professional instead.

"Thank you, Ms. P."

Madeline makes a sound like *pshh*. "Call me Maddie. Please."

"Maddie," I say, tasting Mom's nickname for the first time in months. It's bittersweet.

I tell Maddie that I'll keep her informed, and then walk back toward Gus. Halfway there, Marley intercepts me, running barefoot through the grass.

"My mom said you came by," she says, out of breath.

"Just for a second." I skip past the topic as fast as

possible. "I was going to talk to the guest in Flamingo House and thought you might want to come with me. Good news—she's okay with the picnic."

Marley stares at her lavender-painted toenails. "Cool. But, like, did my mom say anything to you?"

Just that your dad had secret credit cards and an affair.

"Not really," I say.

Her face makes it clear that she doesn't believe me. She laces her fingers together.

"She's miserable. And can't stop telling everyone exactly *why* she's miserable. It makes it too easy for people to talk about us." She takes a deep breath. I hope the lake air will clear whatever is happening in her head. "I never stood a chance in Lincoln."

"Things can get better," I say, even though sometimes I'm not totally convinced they can.

Marley rolls her eyes. "It feels like I don't even have my mom anymore."

My heart snaps and my head clouds up. How can she say that, when her mom is still here, inside Skylight House, angry but alive? Dad hasn't come out, so I walk away from Marley and sit on the curb near Gus. Derek was right. I never should have tried to be friends with Bossy Floss.

She sits next to me a few seconds later. Neither of us talks for a minute, and I think we could sit in this quiet until Dad comes outside, neither of us moving. I've felt this way with Calla after a fight. Like just being side by side is apology enough.

"My mom loved Lakefest," I finally say.

Marley nods, and I know she gets it. *Loved* Lakefest.

"Is that why we're bringing it back?" she asks.

"If I can bring it back, then maybe things can be like they were when she was here."

It's a big wish. A wish too big for genies or dandelions, probably too big to come true. Embarrassment wraps around me.

"I'm glad to be a part of it, then," Marley says, like my dream isn't stupid at all. "I'm sort of doing the same thing with our insect project."

I shift to face her on the curb, curl one knee into my chest.

"What do you mean?"

Marley copies my position. "Did you wonder why I picked a cockroach?" she asks.

"It actually has been . . . bugging me," I say. Marley's cheeks puff out and she breaks into her honk-laugh. Any tension left between us floats away.

She wipes under her eyes. "In our old house, before we moved to Lincoln, we had a cockroach infestation. The exterminators had to come and we couldn't be home. So we went and stayed at this little hotel on the beach. It was the best week I can remember. My parents were so happy, and I was so happy, and we did nothing but collect seashells and eat lobster rolls for five days. I appreciate the cockroaches for giving me those memories."

This whole time we've been helping each other relive our favorite moments, and we didn't even know it.

"I'm happy to be a part of your project too."

Marley stands at the same time the door opens at Fireplace House. We say goodbye, and she runs back across the lawn. Dad stands on the porch with the Realtor, who waves at me like I'm five.

I wave, then stick my tongue out at him as soon as he looks away.

CHAPTER TWENTY-FOUR

THE REAL ERROR

The Lions' game against the Bashers is the next day. Coach Tanaka has us huddle together in the dugout before warm-ups. I'm in my shin guards and chest protector. The gear works to protect me from pitches, but it also keeps all the jitters inside, my feet on the ground. Like being under a weighted blanket.

"The Blossom Bakery Warriors won their semifinal game," Coach Tanaka says. He has his stats book in his hands. "Whoever wins this game plays them in the championship. Who do we want that to be?"

"Us!" we chant back.

"It's yours. Take it," Coach says. "Now go warm up."

We jog to the outfield and split into pairs. Lily automatically lines up across from me. My teammates toss balls back and forth while I'm crouched down, waiting for Lily to take her first practice pitch. She picks at the end of her blond braid.

"I can't wait for Lakefest," Aimi says next to me. She's warming up with Sophia, who nods in agreement across from us. I look away from Lily. She still seems more focused on her split ends than on softball.

"I'm so glad you're coming." Some of the nerves in my stomach ease up. *Someone* is going to be there.

"Can we not talk about your stupid picnic? No one cares." Lily seems ready to pitch now. Or throw me off a cliff or something. Her sharp words come so sudden and quick, it knocks the breath out of me. Aimi tosses the ball back to Sophia with her jaw dropped.

How can Lily's comment make me want to call the whole thing off? Should I really think Lakefest is lame just because Lily Graham said so? Or should I remember that the picnic brings laughs and memories and first kisses, and there's nothing lame about that at all?

I open my mitt and squeeze it, showing that I'm ready. "Pitch, then."

Twenty minutes later we're listening to a staticky speaker play the national anthem, and the game begins. We're the home team, which means the Bashers are up to bat first. I jog to my place behind home plate. Dad and Calla sit together in the stands. My hopes to make them proud settle on my shoulders.

Lily goes to the pitcher's mound, draws lines in the dirt that match the worried squiggles in her forehead. The first Basher comes to the plate. I wait for Lily to stop pacing and give me her ready signal. Her first pitch is hard and fast, but way too high. I have to stand to catch it. The next one is even higher, and the last one ends up in the dirt. I squeeze my knees together to stop it. The number one job of a catcher is to keep the ball in front of you. Using whatever body part necessary.

The second job is to communicate with your pitcher. Even if she bruised your feelings a few minutes ago.

I call a time-out to the umpire and meet Lily on the mound.

"What are you doing?" she asks. Her face is shiny with sweat.

"You seem off," I say. A small shiver runs up my spine. I'm insulting the queen.

"Oh, do I?" Her voice is so sarcastic, I flinch.

I narrow my eyes, let the anger fill my head and my heart. We're *teammates*. It's her job as the pitcher to act like it.

"Look, maybe you feel like you can talk down to me because you're Lily and you're popular and perfect, but we're a unit here, okay? For six innings."

Her crystal-blue eyes fill up.

"I'm nervous, Brooke," she says. She kicks her heel against the rubber mound and it makes a bouncy sound. One tear slides down her cheek. "I *have* to win."

Watching her cry feels like overhearing a private conversation. I want to run before anyone catches me, but at the same time I want to know more. The Basher twirls her bat as she waits outside the box. *J&B Funeral Home* is scripted on the front of her jersey. I prepare for a stab of grief, but it doesn't come. Maybe because Mom wouldn't want me to feel sad on a softball field.

"Wrap it up," the umpire commands from home plate.

Lily blinks a few times. She looks at me like she's waiting for an answer I don't have.

"My mom gave me a lot of softball advice." I pause, expecting her to roll her eyes and tell me *never mind*, but she doesn't. "There was one thing she said to me the most: *It's just a game.*"

Her eyes dry up and turn determined.

"Thanks. And . . . I'm sorry."

The umpire whistles. I rush back to the plate before he can warn us again. I squat in position, and before I drop my mask, I mouth *just a game* to Lily. She lifts her glove to her face and nods.

The Basher steps up to the plate again, and the umpire reminds us it's three balls, no strikes. Lily smiles over her glove. Her pitch goes right down the middle, and the next two are just as good. *Strike three, you're out.* The next batter meets the same fate. With two outs and no one on base, Kasey steps up to the plate. She sticks her tongue out at me.

"Watch this," she says, then gets into position.

We are definitely not in Mrs. Valencia's class anymore.

I give Lily the signal for a changeup. She nods, and I swear I see her mouth *just a game.* The ball comes slowly out of her hand. At first, I think it's going to fool Kasey. But then she waits, waits, for the pitch to cross the plate. She swings, and the ball blasts off her bat and into the air, into the deep part of center field. Sophia runs backward, but it's already over her head. She picks up speed to grab it where it lands near the fence.

"Keep running!" the Bashers coach shouts to Kasey while she rounds first and then second. Sophia has the ball now and is sprinting back in. She throws it to Lily just as Kasey rounds third, making her way to home plate.

Lily throws it to me when Kasey is a foot away. It's a tough throw, too far to my right, and I end up in a split trying to stop it. The ball collides with the bony part of my ankle. I curl up, gripping my foot, the pain like an explosion.

"Safe!" the umpire announces as Kasey slides in for her home run.

I press my foot into the ground, and the weight makes my ankle scream. Lily and Aimi rush to my side, with Coach Tanaka close behind.

"Are you okay?" Aimi asks.

"It's my ankle," I say through my teeth. We're losing and I'm injured and all I want to do is cry.

"I threw it so badly. I'm sorry, Brooke," Lily says. She bites her bottom lip.

"I'll be fine." I try to stand again, but the pain is too sharp and I crumple. Lily and Aimi bend down, put one of my arms around each of their necks, and lift. I hop on one foot to the dugout while they carry me.

"You have two minutes, Coach," the umpire says.

The game can't stop just because I'm hurt. Softball doesn't work that way. Well, I guess life doesn't work that way. Coach Tanaka calls Sophia in from center field to take over as catcher. Lily and Aimi help me sit on the bench and then hustle back out to their positions.

Coach Tanaka kneels in front of me and removes my cleat. My ankle aches too much for me to worry how sweaty my sock must be in his hand. He gently rolls my foot from side to side.

"How does that feel?" he asks.

"Bad," I say.

"What's your pain level? Scale of one to ten." He points

and flexes my foot. The point doesn't hurt too bad, but the flex feels like fire.

"Like a six."

Dad rushes into the dugout, Calla close behind.

"Brookie. Are you all right?" Dad asks.

Hot tears sting my eyes. I can't make my voice work, so I just nod. Dad steps close enough to put his hand on my shoulder. Coach Tanaka keeps moving my foot in different directions.

I look down at the bench, and my pain level reaches a thousand. Coach Tanaka's folder sits next to me, with the slip that I forged right on top. Dad stares straight at "his" signature.

"What is that?" he asks.

Coach Tanaka looks where he's pointing. "Her emergency authorization form." He releases my foot. "I don't think she'll need an ambulance, though. Seems like a sprain, no breaks."

Dad glares at me. Whatever sympathy he had for my injury has disappeared.

"Should we take her home?" Calla asks.

Coach Tanaka pops an ice pack from the first-aid kit. He hands it to me, and I shake it until it turns cold. As cold as my insides feel. As cold as Dad's eyes.

"Ice will do it. She can stay and watch the rest." Coach holds his fist out. "You're a tough Lion, Dell."

I fist-bump him with my ice-pack hand.

"We're taking her home," Dad says.

The umpire gives his warning whistle. Coach Tanaka looks back and forth between me and the field.

"No problem. We'll try to get this win for you." He rushes to tell the umpire that our team is ready to go.

Dad walks out fast, leaving Calla and me behind in the dugout.

"What's going on?" she asks.

I shake my head, test my ankle again. The weight still hurts, but not as much. I limp out of the dugout, holding Calla's shoulder with one hand and my ice pack with the other. The sounds of the game start up again. Balls slapping gloves, the Bashers cheering for their batter. It's like nothing happened, like my huge mistake with the permission slip wasn't exposed.

Softball Error #3. Maybe the worst of them all.

Gus's door is open, and the passenger seat is leaned forward so I can get into the back. I feel like a criminal being put into a police car. Calla helps me get settled with my leg stretched out and the ice pack in the right place while Dad watches in the rearview mirror.

We ease out of the parking lot, then onto the street.

"Who signed that form, Brooke?" Dad finally asks.

I'm drowning in a sea of missed assignments, dirty laundry, broken promises to be better. Why can't I just be good, like Mom always told me to be?

"I signed it."

Calla turns in the passenger seat to look at me, her mouth open.

Dad squeezes the steering wheel.

"You're grounded. Unless you are doing something for Lakefest, which you have already made a commitment to." He pulls up to a stoplight, and the red glow fills the car. "And once Lakefest is over? You're double grounded."

CHAPTER TWENTY-FIVE

OVERWHELMED

D ad's never been good at sticking with his punishments. It was Mom who would make sure Calla and I were disciplined. Which is why I'm downstairs the night of the game, with the TV on and my cell phone nearby.

But he is good at the silent treatment. Which is ten times worse than no electronics. It was the fear of disappointing Dad that made me forge the signature, yet here we are, disappointment filling our whole split-apart house.

I lie on my stomach on the couch, my forehead pressed into the cushion. I should be doing my homework, or confirming the menu with La Manzana, like Marley asked me to, but I can't move from my loglike position. I was nuts to think I'd be able to handle all this. Something always slips through the cracks with me. This situation with the permission slip just proves it.

My phone buzzes on the table, next to my half-finished vocabulary worksheet. I lift my head to look at it. It's Derek.

B, it's been two days, we need to talk. Text me back, please.

My head drops back to the pillow. The TV plays a sports movie I haven't watched since Mom died. I want to mute it, but then I'd have to move.

The phone buzzes again. I groan and look. Marley.

Did you confirm with the market?

Another buzz. Our Lions group chat.

"Is this a joke?" I say out loud, to no one.

Next stop, championships!
Let's go Lions!

Buzz.

B, are you there? I want to give you space, but I need to apologize to you.

Buzz.

Also do you know if Robby has his own extension cord?

"Argh!"

I sit up, grab my phone from its spot next to my unfinished English homework, and whip it across the room. It thuds against the wall before dropping to the floor, finally silent.

"What's wrong?" Calla shouts down the stairs.

"Nothing!" I answer too harshly, because I mean *everything*.

My breath comes back, slow and heavy.

"Hey, you." I hear a voice that isn't Calla's. I scan the room for something supernatural. *"Yeah. You."*

It's coming from my phone. I stand and walk slowly toward the wall, my ankle still tender and throbbing.

"I have something to share with you."

I pick up my phone, thankful not to see any cracks. The video app has opened itself to Organizer Olivia. She has one hand cupped around her pink glossy mouth, like she's going to tell me a secret.

"Did you know I make my living off being organized? Of course you do. That's why you're here."

I take my phone back to the couch, eyes glued to Olivia. I've been watching her videos ever since Marley had me take the quiz. But I haven't seen this one.

"Do you know what my room looks like right now? Let me show you."

She flips her camera around to face a room with pale peach walls. A white comforter is clumped at the bottom of her bed. The floor is covered with towels and books, and all the dresser drawers are open. Clothes pop out like jack-in-the-boxes.

Her face comes into focus again.

"That's right. It's a mess! Nothing that looks perfect really is, darlings. So don't hold yourself to that standard."

She gives her sign-off, and the video ends.

Nothing has really changed. Dad is still mad, and I don't know what to say to Derek, and my vocabulary sheet still isn't done. But if Organizer Olivia says I don't have to be perfect, then maybe all I have to do is try my best.

I take a deep breath and dial the number for La Manzana.

CHAPTER TWENTY-SIX

SEVENTH-INNING STRETCH

E ven grounded people have to eat dinner. Calla calls me to help set the table, and I walk up the stairs with my legs heavy and my heart racing. The plates are stacked next to a blue bowl of Caesar salad. I take them, circle the table to put one at each spot. Dad is on the couch in the living room, watching an Orioles game and frowning. He doesn't look at me.

"Dinner's ready, Dad," Calla says softly. She puts the salad bowl in the center of the table.

He gets up, groaning the way Grandpa Ed used to when he stood. Like he's aged twenty years all of a sudden. I fight the tight feeling in my throat, my body's signal that I'm about to cry. The kitchen is full to the brim with awkward silence when we sit and take servings of the salad. I swirl the soggy lettuce around on the plate.

"It's the seventh-inning stretch, folks," the announcer declares.

An organ starts playing "Take Me Out to the Ball Game." It's Dad's favorite part of the game, but he lowers the volume with the remote. This is not what things are supposed to be like three days before Lakefest. The sound of crouton crunching drives me crazy. I slam my fork down on the table.

"I forgot about the form and had to sit out at practice. I didn't want to tell you that I'd messed up another thing, so I made the problem go away. I'm sorry," I explain.

Dad doesn't even lift his head. "How did that work, Brooke? Did your problem go away?"

He's never talked to me so harshly, not even when I dented Gus with a softball.

"She apologized, Dad, andyouhavebeenkindofunavailable, so can we just move on?" Calla blurts.

"What?" Dad asks, his forehead creasing.

But I can translate Calla's speed sentence. The words that could make everything explode.

"We know you have a lot going on," she explains. "And that you're doing your best. But you've been too busy to notice things falling apart around here. We need you."

Dad lays his fork down, stretches a hand over his mouth.

"And you felt like you couldn't tell me that?" he asks.

His eyes shift from Calla to me to the empty chair across the table. Back to Calla.

"You're already stretched so thin, it seemed easier to just pick up the slack. But it's not easy." Calla shakes her head. "It's been really freaking hard."

She looks at me, her eyes searching for backup. I thought Calla was keeping it together this whole time. But she's been struggling, trying to keep the stress off Dad.

By becoming Mom.

"You said you wouldn't be mad if we just told you the truth." I remind Dad of what he told me in the car after seeing those emails from Mrs. Valencia.

Dad's face softens. The sound of applause comes quietly from the TV; I can't totally hear the announcement, but the Orioles did something right.

"The truth just hurts sometimes," Dad says in a crackly voice.

Calla walks to Dad's chair. She wraps her arms around his neck, rests her head on his shoulder. Dad holds on to her elbow and closes his eyes. I come around and take his other side. He makes a short sniffling sound.

"I'll start doing more work from home," he says, and the three of us pull apart. "And what were those boxes, the ones your mom used to help you remember your work?"

"The Do and Done baskets," I answer.

"Right. Let's get those back in action."

Calla rushes to the hall closet, comes back with the two pink baskets. Seeing Mom's handwriting puts a lump in my throat. Calla drops the baskets at the top of the stairs.

"From now on, we *do* start leaning on each other," Dad says.

"Done," Calla and I say at the same time.

CHAPTER TWENTY-SEVEN
APOLOGY APPLE JUICE

On Friday, I sit with Marley in the cafeteria for the third day in a row. The rest of the table is empty today, so we spread our lunches out in front of us like a buffet. We take turns calling off the final details for Lakefest, like when you go on a vacation and make sure you have everything packed.

"Music?" Marley asks.

"Check, Robby has our playlist. Kayaks?"

"Check, I confirmed with the rental place yesterday that they'll drop off two complimentary kayaks. But if anyone breaks them, we'll be buying them."

"Check, guard the kayaks with our lives."

Marley laughs with a mouth full of carrot stick and points over my shoulder.

"Derek's coming," she says.

My heart tries to escape from my chest. I lower my head to the table. He's sent dozens of unanswered texts since that day he almost kissed me, but I never thought he'd approach me in the cafeteria. At Marley's table.

"Are you in a fight?" Marley taps my arm with her carrot stick. "Is that why you've been sitting here?"

"Wealmostkissed." I say it quiet and fast, the way Calla would.

"Huh?"

I lift my head. "We almost kissed!" This time I say it too loud. Some theater kids at the next table over turn their heads.

Derek stands near my shoulder. I'm afraid to look at his face. I don't want to replay the moment when it was an inch from mine. It's like the closer we get to kissing, the closer I am to losing him. What if our friendship can't survive those big, fluttery feelings?

Calla and Robby didn't.

"That's kind of what I want to talk to you about," Derek says.

Marley gathers up her lunch and stands.

"I'll go," she says.

"You can stay, Marley. If you want." Derek sits next to me.

I finally turn toward him. He's okay with people seeing him sit here?

"You should have some privacy." She shuffles to another empty table, and then it's just me and Derek.

He reaches into the front pocket of his hoodie and puts a tall bottle of apple juice on the table in front of me.

"What's that for?" I ask.

"I didn't think an emergency slushie was the right choice." He nudges the juice closer to me. "So I'm trying an apology apple juice. Please don't be mad at me."

I laugh in a spluttery way that almost sounds like crying. Because Derek can always make me laugh, and I was never really angry at him. I was just scared. Running felt easier than saying it out loud.

"I'm not mad at you, D."

A smile splits his face. His eyes are so bright, and his curls are so cute, and . . .

Stop! This is where the trouble started in the first place! It's Derek. Best friend. Derek.

"I was so worried you would never speak to me again. I thought I had pressured you, and I felt horrible about it. I was so nervous, I ate an entire bag of sunflower seeds. And not even a good flavor."

Oh.

Wait.

It's Derek.

Derek, who was worried about pressuring me. Derek,

who would never say things like those boys at the concession stand. Derek, my best friend, who makes me feel like hearts can hit home runs.

Of course I would want to kiss someone like that.

And despite those boys calling me a two at the snack stand, Derek wanted to kiss me, too.

But not here in the cafeteria, of course. I unscrew the top on the apology apple juice and take a long forgiveness sip.

CHAPTER TWENTY-EIGHT

MANiPULATi⊘N

The day before Lakefest is the hottest of the year so far. Calla and I sit on the deck with glasses of lemonade and her podcast playing in the background. Something exciting must have happened in the last episode, because the hosts won't stop squealing.

"Are you nervous for the picnic?" she asks.

My heart has been racing for most of the day. Last night I dreamt that the lake dried up entirely, and we had to kayak in the dirt left behind.

"No one is going to show up," I say.

Calla taps my shin with her sandal.

"That's impossible. I've already heard that a bunch of people from student council and Spanish club are coming. And Derek, and the Lions, and everyone who goes to Papa Margherita's. Lincoln will support you."

I like the idea of the whole town being on my team.

"I'm just happy you'll be there," I tell her.

"Consider me your official banker."

Calla does a motion like she's rubbing dollar bills between her fingers. She volunteered to collect the entrance fee from the guests. Dad's going to help with the food and kayaks. Derek, Marley, and I are the Fun Committee, there to make sure everyone has a good time.

Calla's phone vibrates on the table, silencing her podcast. I can't help but see the name on her screen. *Robby.*

I look away, toward the trees. I have a million questions, but I swallow them all. Calla snorts and picks up her phone.

"I know you saw that. We're talking a little bit."

Maybe just one question would be okay.

"Are you getting back together?" I ask.

"We haven't discussed that yet. But him helping you, even though I did what I did, made me remember how kind he really is." She takes a breath. "I miss him."

She says it without shoving the words together. It's her truth, one word at a time. My heart just about explodes.

"I knew it would work!"

Calla looks puzzled. "What do you mean?"

Sweat pools under my arms. The temperature is too hot for May. We need to reassemble Mega Float.

"I thought that if he helped with Lakefest, you might want him to be your boyfriend again."

I see every feeling cross Calla's face. No glued-on smile, no hyper-speed speech. There's pain and anger and tears in her eyes. And it's all my fault.

"How could you manipulate me that way?" Her voice sounds clogged.

"I didn't think of it like that, Calla, I swear."

"That's the problem. You don't think." She stabs her finger into the side of her head. "How about you start being responsible for your own stuff so I don't have to be? Because I'm getting pretty sick of it."

Calla isn't Mom. Even if she's been acting like it. And in my attempt to change her back to the way she was before, I've hurt her the way that only sisters can hurt each other.

"I'll do better," I mumble.

The wooden chair legs scrape the deck when Calla stands.

"Have a great time tomorrow, Brooke."

The backyard and house blur together. Maybe my dream was right and the lake really did dry up, because everything is wrong, wrong, wrong.

"You're not going to come?" I ask the back of Calla's head.

She slams the screen door.

CHAPTER TWENTY-NINE

LAKEFEST

On Lakefest day, Derek, Marley, and I sit at a table in Purple Couch House's yard, the first house that guests will see when they drive into the circle. We spent the last hour spreading red-checkered tablecloths, dragging kayaks to the lake, putting orange cones out to mark parking spaces. I've been sucking down lake air the whole time, but it's not enough to clear out my thoughts about Calla. She slept downstairs last night. I turned her night-lights on, just in case she came back to our room, but she didn't.

Robby has his DJ equipment set up under a tree. He keeps looking around the lawns, and I avoid his eyes, because I know he won't find who he's looking for.

A white van with *La Manzana* written inside an apple pulls up to the curb. Benito the butcher steps out. He's wearing all black, including his apron and work boots.

"Brooke Dell?" he calls out.

I join him in the front yard.

"That's me," I tell him.

"Half our equipment busted this morning." He wipes sweat off his forehead. "I only have some of your food."

My nightmare has leaked into real life. I turn around, just to make sure the lake is still full of water.

"How much do you have?"

Benito guides me to the back of the van. He opens the double doors, and two aluminum trays sit in a cardboard box.

"I have one tray of arroz con habichuelas and one of pollo sofrito."

I try to stay logical. Even if La Manzana didn't bring enough food, we still have Papa Margherita's, right? If we put a one-slice limit on the pizza, then everyone will get something to eat.

Maybe.

"That's okay. Thank you for bringing what you have. We really appreciate it."

Benito rolls his lips together and nods. "I won't charge you for this either." He takes the trays and follows me to the backyard. I tell him where to set them down, before he goes to talk to Robby. The buffet table looks painfully empty.

"What happened?" Derek asks.

"Technical difficulties," I say, and turn to Marley. "What should we do?"

Marley's mouth opens and closes, but no instruction comes out.

"I don't know," she says.

We're doomed.

The sound of a sliding door pulls me from my worries. Dad comes down the back steps of Flamingo House, wearing a Hawaiian shirt. A long orange extension cord ropes around his arm. He drops it off to Robby before joining us.

"Why the long faces? It's picnic day!" Dad's enthusiasm lifts my spirits for a second. He looks like he's jumped out of the Lakefest photo album.

"We're not going to have enough food. Even with the pizza," I tell him.

Dad looks unbothered by the news. His eyes shift over my shoulder.

"You forgot something else about Lakefest," he says.

Robby's music starts up, a song about celebrating good times.

"What?" the three of us ask at the same time.

"The people."

He points and we turn. Cars stream into the circle and find parking spots on the side of the road. Groups are starting to get out and walk onto the lawns. Most of them hold trays in their hands, like the ones from La Manzana but smaller. They drop their contributions onto the table and then find spots in the grass, spreading out picnic blankets and lawn chairs. Soon the buffet table is overflowing with casseroles and cookies.

"Welcome back, Lakefest!" someone shouts. I recognize Coach Tanaka's voice. He walks over with Aimi and Mrs. Tanaka. Aimi has her glove and two Wiffle ball bats.

"Like we never left!" Dad calls back. He looks at us. "Thank you for this, you three."

A feeling too big to describe swells in my chest.

"You're welcome, Dad."

"Wait," Marley says. "We haven't taken any entry fees. What are we going to do?"

Her question reminds me that Calla is missing from the crowd. Our fee taker isn't here.

"Don't charge anyone for Lakefest," Dad says. "People pay by showing up. We'll handle any costs. Now go join the party."

We do what he says. For the next three hours, we play Wiffle ball with kids from the junior leagues, eat more food than our stomachs can handle, listen to Robby play song after song. I see Madeline P moving through the crowd, handing out tiny cups of tea. Poppyseed has their truck parked in front of Fireplace House, and Lily and her friends buy flowers to stick in their hair. At one point Lily asks to talk to Marley alone, which probably scares me as much as Marley. But when Marley comes back, she tells me that Lily apologized for the drawing.

Dr. Macintosh is even there, in a yellow jumpsuit. She brings a tray of strawberry cupcakes and adds them to the buffet table, then stands nervously at the edge of the party. Mrs. Tanaka swoops in and guides her over to a group of softball moms at a shady picnic table.

I'm at the buffet with a fudgy brownie in my mouth when someone taps my shoulder. I turn, and Calla is there in a blue dress with buttons down the front.

"Hi," she says.

My mouth is practically glued shut with chocolate. I struggle to swallow. Calla watches me the whole time with her nose wrinkled.

"You're here," I finally say.

She shrugs and turns toward the yard. "It looks just like I remember."

"I didn't think you would come," I add.

"I didn't think I would either." She looks out to the lawn. "But then I would have missed that."

I follow her gaze. Dad is bent backward, shimmying under a limbo stick. Coach Tanaka holds one end and Jensen the other. He emerges on the other side in a fit of laughter. I can't remember the last time I saw him this happy.

"You did good, Brooke," she says. Her face doesn't look like she's forgiven me. Some things may take more than a town picnic to fix. But she's *here*. And that was supposed to be the point, right?

Something pushes against my heart. This is Lakefest, but it's not a perfect replica of how the old picnics were. And on my mission to re-create the past, I betrayed Calla.

Maybe things don't have to be the same to still be good.

Maybe we can be happy now, even if Mom isn't here.

Maybe I don't need to hold on so tight to these houses.

Maybe it's okay to let go.

It's late, and Lakefest is over. We've scoured the lawns with big black trash bags and pulled the kayaks to shore. Calla even helped. She wouldn't say more than a few words at a time to me, but still. Robby stayed too. He orbited Calla like a moon, never getting too close, while they cleaned up forgotten towels and coolers. When they were finished, I saw them walk toward the street, disappearing around the house. I have no way to know if they'll kiss good night or never speak to each other again.

It isn't my decision to make.

Dad sits in a chair on Flamingo House's deck with

Madeline P. I wonder what kind of character she would write based on Dad. Maybe the goofy hero, or a brave knight.

I'm with Derek on the end of the dock.

"We did it, B," Derek says.

I feel warm and sun-kissed, even in the dark, like the happiness of today is still on my skin. Or maybe it's because Derek's shoulder is less than an inch from mine, and our legs are even closer. We've been in this position a few times now. Although tonight, I'm not scared. I turn to the side, lean in as close as the day I ran away from him.

"This feels special, right?" I ask.

Derek nods really fast, and our lips touch. For one second, then two, then three. I can feel his smile and taste waxy ChapStick. We sit back again, and stack our hands on top of each other on the dock. The world feels totally different and exactly the same.

And all I want to do is tell Calla.

CHAPTER THIRTY

THE GARDEN

I jolt out of sleep that night to the sound of something moving in the front yard. My phone on the dresser says it's after two in the morning.

"Calla," I whisper, but of course her bed is empty. She slept downstairs again.

The sound outside continues. I ease out from under my comforter and tiptoe to the window. Outside, Calla is kneeling by her garden, stabbing her trowel into the dirt again and again. She grips a full tomato plant by its stem and yanks it from the ground.

I rush out of the room, down the stairs of our split-apart house. I'm quiet when I open the door and slip through. The air is cold, and the wet grass sticks to my feet. When I'm close enough, I can hear Calla's sobs mixed in with the digging sounds. She hacks at a cluster of violets, the ones she planted after our trip to Poppyseed.

I sit down next to her, ignore the dew seeping through my pajama pants.

"Let me help you," I say.

She looks over at me, collapses, lands with her head in my lap. I let my big sister cry into her flowers like she did on her first day of T-ball. She shivers while I rub her arm.

When she's done, she sits with her knees tucked to her chest. She doesn't go back to destroying her garden.

"I'm sorry for what I did," I say.

Calla nods.

"I love Robby," she says. "But people we love go away. My heart can't handle any more of that right now, and talking to him today only proved that." She looks at me. "You should've understood that better than anyone."

So Lakefest didn't reunite her and Robby. Because Calla isn't ready for that, and I can't squeeze her into some mold of who she used to be when Mom was here. She isn't that person anymore.

"You seemed so fine. You took over everything so easily."

Calla shakes her head, fills in one of the holes she made. "It's not easy."

I thought she was trying to replace Mom, but *I'm* the one who wasn't acting like a sister. Instead of resenting how busy she was, begrudging the way she stressed over junior year and decided to break up with Robby, I should have been cheering her on.

I help Calla replant what she ripped out of the ground, and then we sit in the grass under the stars for a while. I wonder if she'll go back downstairs, but when we get inside, she doesn't split apart from me in the entryway. We tiptoe together through the dark house, to our room glowing softly from Calla's string lights.

CHAPTER THIRTY-ONE

WE PROUDLY PRESENT COCKROACH

Marley and I have our cockroach presentation on Wednesday. We're the second group up, after Aimi, Kasey, and Larissa, who giggle their way through their poster on fire ants.

"Brooke, Marley, it's your time to shine," Mrs. Valencia says.

We head to the front of the class. Marley props our poster board up on the presentation table. In the center is a picture of a cockroach with its brown body and twiggy antennas.

"We learned a lot about cockroaches through this project," Marley begins. "Their life span is one to two years. There are almost five thousand different species of cockroaches worldwide. And, of course, you don't want to find them in your house."

That line makes some of our classmates laugh, which is what we planned for.

She turns to me. Her smile is shaky. It's my turn to talk.

"We also found some unexpected information, about the symbolism of a cockroach infestation." I look at the left side of the poster board. Marley wrote this part in a heart-shaped box. I point to the top. "They represent resilience."

"'Overcoming obstacles,'" Marley reads, continuing down the list.

I clear my throat. "And transformation."

We go through the rest of our cockroach facts, and the class applauds in the polite way they have to. I fold the poster board up and go sit with Marley in her spot by the window. We watch the rest of our classmates' presentations and walk together to our lockers after the bell rings.

"I totally messed up on our speech," Marley says.

The surprise is like a static shock. I thought the presentation went great. Well, as great as any oral report can go.

"I didn't notice," I answer.

Marley shrugs. I think about the Organizer Olivia video that made me feel better when I was overwhelmed.

"You know you don't have to be perfect, right?" I tell her.

Marley half smiles with shiny eyes. For a second I think she might hug me.

"I know," she answers. "Do you?"

I used to think I had to be. I thought it was the only way to never disappoint anyone. But it's hard to do everything right all the time.

"Yeah. I know."

CHAPTER THIRTY-TWO

THE CIRCLE

The championship game is a week after Lakefest. We trail the Blossom Bakery Warriors by one run for all six innings. But not because we aren't playing our best. Lily and I are in sync, and the whole team is hitting better than we have all season. Aimi is up next to bat, with runners on first and third. It's the most stressful situation a softball player can be in—the game on the line, the team on your shoulders. I'm in my Disaster Corner, which I'm thinking about just calling My Corner now, when I see Aimi freeze near the fence a few feet from the plate.

"It's just a game!" Lily calls to her.

I smile, and Aimi smiles, and her long braids bounce on the way to the batter's box.

I stand at the fence with my teammates. It seems like no one is breathing when the Warrior pitcher winds her arm back and sends a fastball straight down the center of home plate.

Aimi draws her arms back a little, and then swings. Her bat smacks the ball with a loud, perfect *ping*. We watch it fly higher and farther through the air. It lands at the very edge of the fence, where a Warrior has to dig it out. But by that time, our two other runners have already made it home, with Aimi sprinting in right behind them.

The winning runs. We win.

Coach Tanaka treats us to a round of victory ice cream at the concession stand. Family and friends, too. I have Dad and Calla licking vanilla soft serve on one side of me, and Derek close by on the other. I watch him catch a melting trail of chocolate on the edge of his sugar cone. The warm-and-fuzzies fill my chest. There have been a few more kisses since the first one. But other than that, things are the same in the D and B bubble, with Orioles games and catch in the yard and grocery hunts in La Manzana.

The memorial sign for Mom sparkles in the sun, and it doesn't hurt to see her name etched into the metal. It makes me feel like she's here, serving snacks behind the counter with a big smile on her face.

I'm a sweaty, exhilarated lump in Gus's back seat on our way home. Dad drives with the window down, and Calla is beside him, the way they sat on the bleachers during my game.

"How about a detour?" Dad suggests. He takes a left before we can answer, and the compass in my heart spins around, knowing we're headed for the lake.

Calla turns to look at me, smiling.

"Sounds good to me," I say.

The lake appears on my left a few turns later, the blue all sparkling and stretching to infinity and beyond. I want to stare at it and jump in at the same time.

Dad turns into Lakeside Circle and drives slowly past the houses. Purple Couch House, then Fireplace, then Flamingo. Each one has a FOR SALE sign planted in the front yard, with pink flowers from Poppyseed at its base. A few days after Lakefest, Dad said that selling the houses should be a family decision. It made my heart feel sore around the edges, but we all agreed. Letting them go will give us more time to be a family.

We made one exception: the sign in front of Skylight House says FOR RENT.

But it won't be on Rent It. After Marley and her mom's stay ends in a few days, it will be available as a permanent rental house. A place where people can actually live. Where they can watch the stars under the skylight without having to leave the next day.

"Nice day in the circle," Calla says.

Dad smiles at her for stealing his saying.

A million things well up in my chest. I'm sad and scared and happy all at the same time. But right here, right now, it really is a nice day in the circle.

We finish our lap around the lake, and head for home.

ACKNOWLEDGMENTS

The process of writing *This Close to Home* was special and difficult and joyful in so many ways. I'm so thankful to Krista Vitola for being there to help me tug at the threads of early drafts until it became the book about sisterhood and community and change that I hoped it could be. Thank you to the whole team at Simon & Schuster Books for Young Readers for your care in everything from copyediting to the beautiful cover; I could not love the illustration and design by Laura Catrinella and Lizzy Bromley more.

So many thanks to Zoe Sandler for all your support on this journey!

I dedicated this book to my parents because they have filled my life with so many things that became the heart of this book—softball, the Orioles, and a place to call home. I am so lucky to have you, parents. Shout-out to my sister, Cristina, for being a great teammate.

To the rest of my cheering section: my family, my friends, the writing community at Western Connecticut State University. I am so grateful for you all.

I couldn't write a book about lake houses without thanking the Lake House Crew—our memories were the perfect inspiration. Joe, so much of my support in writing this book came from you. Thank you for being my favorite person to be with by the water—and just about everywhere else.

Thank you to every reader who picks up Brooke's story. I hope she makes you believe that you can do anything.

ABOUT THE AUTHOR

Beth Turley is a graduate of the MFA in creative and professional writing program at Western Connecticut State University. She lives and writes in southeastern Connecticut, where the leaves changing color feels like magic and the water is never too far away. She is the author of *If This Were a Story*, *The Last Tree Town*, *The Flyers*, and *This Close to Home*. Visit her on Twitter @Beth_Turley.